DONT MEAN NOTHIN

NOTHIN

VIETNAM WAR STORIES

Other Books by John Mort

Fiction

Tanks

The Walnut King and Other Stories

Soldier in Paradise

Goat Boy of the Ozarks

Nonfiction

Christian Fiction: A Guide to the Genre

Read the High Country: A Guide to Western Books and Films

Dont Mean Nothin

Vietnam War Stories by

John Mort

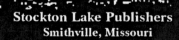

Stockton Lake Publishers
Smithville, Missouri

This collection is fiction. Names, characters, places, and incidents are either the product of the author's imagination or are used fictitiously.

ISBN: 978-0615459912 <> LCCN: 2011933614

Requests to reproduce material from this book should be made to Stockton Lake Publishers, PO Box 976, Smithville, MO 64089.

"Called of God" and "Incubation Period" first appeared in *GQ*, "The New Captain" in *Missouri Review,* "Hallelujah By and By" in *Sou'wester,* "Rest Stop" in *New Letters,* "Behind Enemy Lines" in *Big Muddy,* and "Hot" in the anthology, *Missouri Short Fiction.*

"Good Blood," "Hot," "Human Wave," "Tanks," and the "The New Captain" were collected in *Tanks,* from BkMk Press.

"Hallelujah By and By," "Rest Stop," and "Incubation Period" appeared in *The Walnut King,* from Woods Colt Press.

Many thanks for the cover photo, from Richard Hokenson, which is of Al Rackley and his gunner, Richard Lingers. The back cover is courtesy of Tim Hall; and Wayne Bartunek contributed the helicopter photo introducing "My Vietnam." All of these men served with C/2/8, First Cavalry.

Contents

<<>>

In memory of the soldiers who died on
Valentine's Day, 1970

Good Blood

"LOOKS LIKE, if they was gonna have a war, they'd try to win it," Roy's father said.

"Oh, Jesus. Will you stop it? I don't wanta hear this!" They were out in the chicken house, so early the chickens still slept. Down at the end, through the screen, Roy saw the first streaks of sunlight on his Chevy, forlorn by the dark woods. His father stood before the great ventilation fan with its slowly-moving blades, so that he was alternately in golden outline, and shadow.

"It's this damn Johnson," the old man said. "You can't trust a Texan."

"Just . . . don't talk. Please."

"Had a Texan workin' for me once, name a Phelps. Never sober. Now his wife, she was a different story. Real pretty. And a hard worker."

"Not like my mom?"

Roy's mother had gone to California with a man when Roy was seven. He'd never understand it. But even this knife in the old wound wasn't enough to silence his father. "Phelps got fallin' down drunk one night, and beat her up. Pretty bad. She went on home to Texas, and he moped around somethin' to behold. He had eyes like a hound dog. Man couldn't help but feel sorry for him. Well, a few months went by, and he got religion. Swore off the bottle, and damned if he didn't talk her into comin' back. But that's what I mean about a Texan. Johnson would be all right if he'd kick that Kennedy bunch outta there."

"Oh, God. Shut up! You're so . . . *ignorant.*"

His father blinked. Finally, he bent to pick up his basket. "We better throw a little oyster shell, Roy. We been gettin' some soft eggs."

Roy eyed his father neutrally, wondering if he'd really silenced him. He hurried toward the feed room. He didn't mind the work, but it galled him, with the education he had, to listen to his father's foolishness. He set the bucket of oyster shell near the cages, and picked up his basket of eggs.

"You talk about respect," said the old man.

"I didn't!"

"I respect the man does his duty. I know he's a friend a yours, but that Martin boy—"

"Duty! I got trapped. I ran out of money, *Dad.*"

"Jim Martin lied, pure and simple."

"He convinced them. All he said was, all he really said, was that he objected to killing."

"Who don't? In my time they'd a throwed him in jail. Was a missionary's son in town, refused to go, they painted a yellow streak around his house.

Awful thing. He had grounds, religious grounds. But—"

"I'm going to Canada," Roy announced.

His father nodded. "You won't. I'm gonna tell you why you won't."

"Not that. Not—"

"Because there's good blood in you. Good bull, he'll bring up the herd. You take, little runt of a bull, he's gonna bring it down, I don't care how nice your heifers are. You're like me, Roy, you—"

"Maybe I'm like my mother!" Roy spun like a discus thrower, moaning, ready as he might ever be to kill, and released his basket of eggs. They crashed into the wall and yolks slid down the calendar from Biggs Feed Mill, the one with the girl in pigtails. He ran outside. A wind had come up, and it was cold.

The old man bustled about inside, making loud, improbable noises. Finally he emerged, jingling his keys, looking into his billfold. "Let's get on the road," he said. "I'll buy you breakfast."

Polly Selznick, who at nineteen already had a kid, and already was divorced, brought their order. In high school Roy never had the nerve to ask her out, but what he thought now was that he'd spent the summer working, lonely, when all the time he could have been seeing Polly. "Roy!" she said, smiling. "Answer to a maiden's prayer."

He scanned her eyes. A different waitress had taken their order, and he wondered if there had been a conference in the kitchen. "Hello, Polly."

"Roy's goin' into the service today," said the old man.

"I hope it's not because of a woman."

Roy slurped his coffee. "Drafted."

"I'm sorry." Polly shook her head. "What a shame, Roy."

"It is," said the old man. "This war don't make no sense. Explain it to me, Polly."

"I guess I just don't pay much attention. Isn't that awful? I know someone over there, too. Get you fellas anything else?"

Roy looked at her carefully. "Might call you some time. When I'm home."

She laughed. "Thought you were interested in college girls."

"I'm interested—" He stopped, compromised by the old man at his shoulder.

"I think Roy may be done with school. Comes right down to it, he's a farmer like me, God help us all."

"*You* say!"

"He should finish up," Polly said. "Sure wish I'd gone."

"He wasn't serious, Polly! I said to him, engineering, even agriculture, that's fine. Welding. Business classes. But he's gonna go up there and paint be-you-tiful pictures, by God, I said, he can pay for it."

"I got bad blood," Roy explained. "Runs in the family."

"Don't argue." Polly glanced toward a table

where Butch Fredericks and Avery Dunn had taken seats. She sighed. "Listen, I'll bring you two some pie. My treat, huh?"

Roy nodded. He wished he had time to fall in love. Strange, but lately, at unexpected moments, he found himself fighting back tears. He watched Polly as she hovered over Butch and Avery—in the national guard, he remembered. He didn't have much of an appetite for pie.

The International rattled along, with an instinct for every bump. His father took some incredible back route, and crunched the gears with every shift. "Learn to drive," Roy said.

"I ain't put it out to pasture yet."

He meant the Chevy. Draft notice in hand, Roy got drunk, ran too hard, and blew his engine. The old man had to tow it home—twenty miles behind the tractor, ten miles an hour. "I screwed up. I know I did. But—"

"We'll get her fixed while you're gone."

Roy couldn't speak. He'd been about to say that the old man couldn't let a sleeping dog lie.

They reached the city. The strange route brought them through the ghetto, behind delivery trucks, by a junkyard, over myriad rail crossings. That sat at a light, and two tall black boys danced in front of a pawn shop. Roy braced himself for the inevitable racial slur. No matter how the old man goaded him, he'd remain calm.

"Speakin' a Polly," his father said.

"Please don't."

"Had some tough luck, that's all. Always mystified me, how these nice women settle on such hard cases. Guess there ain't enough good men to go around. But I tell you somethin', Roy—woman like that, kid to think of, she'll stay with you."

"Not like Mom, huh?"

His father went silent. As they pulled from the light, and the old man crunched into second, the two black boys stepped onto the street. They danced to some secret music, and seemed oblivious to traffic. Here it comes, Roy thought, steeling himself.

The old man braked, and blundered back into first. Then they went on silently for a dozen blocks, over brick streets. An expressway curved parallel to them, and ran over their heads. Suddenly his father was backing the truck around. "I guess this is the place."

"Oh." Roy sat up. "Well . . . goodbye, then." He didn't move.

"Same place they swore me in. Ain't changed a bit. Well—"

Roy looked through the rear window. A bus marked "Chartered" sat under the expressway. A big sergeant strode before a group of twenty or so, in civilian clothes, in haphazard formation.

"I'm going," said Roy.

"The place is yours. It ain't like there's anybody else. Make a farmer outta you yet."

"I don't want it!" Roy said. "I don't want that worthless place!"

"You may change your mind. You get over

there—"

"What do you care? If I'm killed, if my legs are blown off, what do you care? You drove me off!" Roy paused. He almost didn't say it. "Like my mother."

The old man hunched over the wheel. "Get on with you, Roy."

"All right! All right!" Roy opened the door and marched down the street. When he'd gone a hundred feet the sergeant looked up. He had a clipboard. "You belong here?"

Roy turned. His father rolled down the window, and waved, as slowly he gained speed. Roy nodded. He meant to shout out something, to wave back. He rocked up on his heels, but his hands were paralyzed.

Hot

LEON WAS IN THE AIR again. It was only in the air, when his head cooled, that he could think of this life as a cycle. In the air he knew how many days had passed, how many times the birds had picked him up and carried him to an identical place, who he was other than "Leon." The bird dropped suddenly, banking through haze. Almost parallel to the earth, Leon imagined leaping away, free of men and machines, into flight. He'd glide down into one of those deep blue craters, fill his canteens, and march away free . . . the bird skimmed over a wide brown river now, nose down. "Where? Where we going?"

The door gunner—with his helmet on, the radio in his ears—couldn't hear. Unless he faced you, he couldn't read your lips, and anyhow Leon's destination wasn't his problem. The men in the birds were aloof, and a little mysterious with their sticks and gauges. It was as though they flew not from some base but from the heavens, moving round and round in the familiar air, like a freight train repeating its run. Leon stood there, ready to dissolve into vapors, when the machines pounced from the sky. Cold men in clean wool suits: moving parts. Now the gunner turned, and Leon asked again: "Where we going?" The man shrugged.

They dipped into rain, and the rain had sun inside it, orange. The rotors pounded as they banked over a defoliated woods, with thick underbrush. A long field loomed, and a radiance flooded over them. This time, Leon thought. This is the one. So he screamed it: "Is it hot? Is it hot?" Meaning: will they shoot me today, will I lie by the crater full of drugs and dreams, will another helicopter take me away?

The gunner smiled. He sat erect on his perch, and tilted up the machine gun. "Cold," he said at last, drawing out the word. "Cold."

As the company threaded into the darkening brush it was all Leon could do to keep Jackson, his squad leader, in sight. One boot chased the next. His head fell, and weariness bobbed along where sleep was supposed to be. Motion ceased, and he stood helplessly in the downpour as others stretched the hooch, arranged guard, searched out dry matches for cigarettes. He flopped under shelter, rolled himself in his poncho liner. Everything was wet, but he fell asleep immediately, and was uplifted into fever and soft, radiant air.

In the bird around him were his mother and father, his older sister the lawyer, and Susan. The wind tore their words away. "What did you say?" he asked. They all smiled and it seemed natural to be together, riding high, the people he loved and himself. The bird rode over a bank of mist, and the far-off horizon quaked with explosions. He was frightened. "Where we going?" he asked. "Please, where?" Susan pursed her lips in a "No," as though his question were in poor taste, as though he'd violated her trust. He turned to his sister, who shook her head—knowing something, as she always had, that he didn't.

"Shh." It was Jackson. "Hey, man. Your guard. Shh."

The rain thundered a few inches above. He crawled forward, trying to escape.

"What you doin', man?"

"I—"

"You sit right there. And stay awake."

" . . . Anything?"

"That's a negative. You kiddin', in this rain? I catch you sleepin' again, Leon—"

"Not me." He was asleep instantly. From the bright air of his dream, emptied now of people, a place to cruise, he answered Jackson: "Yeah, yeah. I'm awake." He opened his eyes, but couldn't see. It was like that experiment he'd read about, where they blindfolded you, put boxing gloves on you, and enclosed you in a padded chamber, to see what you'd do. You did nothing. You ceased to exist. Better to dream, bask in the wonderful light, fall away like a bomber into radiance.

In the dewy morning Leon discovered a boil under his chin. It throbbed, and already was large as a golf ball. He felt it would keep growing until it ate him up. Afterwards, the men would roll him down the trail.

"I had one of those on my ass," the medic said. "It'll bust."

"I can't go in?"

"The CO won't buy it, Leon. It'll bust. If it don't, come over again, two-three days, and I'll lance it."

Jackson looked at the boil and smiled. "You're losing it, Leon."

"The medic said it would bust."

"You better put in for R. & R. Go to Manila, forget about the whores—just sleep. You're starting to *be* the jungle, man. It's taken root."

"I—"

Jackson sighed. "Want the bad news first?"

"Bad news?"

"You drew the point, and it's a long one. Can you do it?"

"What's the good news?"

"Hang in there, I'll pull your guard tonight."

"Oh."

"You fell asleep again, you know that?"

"I was awake, I—"

"I heard you snorin', man."

Leon backed into a tree, to take the pack's weight from his shoulders, and took a long drink. He massaged the boil, under his whiskers and hot skin; it mashed and moved slightly, like clay, but then oozed back to its former shape. Cancer? So young, to die of cancer. He took the weight of the pack again, staggered, plodded on.

Some part of him was still conscious of the temperature, the vagrant sounds, the treacherous path ahead. He stayed on azimuth. He detoured open areas and nests of fire ants. There was a mood to the brush, a level of tolerable menace, and if you were properly attuned you could sense a change, and know when to duck.

For a while he managed, but then he was back with Susan, down by the lake. Her parents came to the door, and she hurried to gather her clothes, he his . . . he fingered the boil, and squinted ahead, and knew where he was again.

He stepped onto a broad trail the map hadn't shown. It was of hard-packed clay and he saw fresh bicycle tracks. As it occurred to him he should consult Jackson, an enemy soldier rounded a curve, and instinctively, Leon raised his rifle. The safety was off and his finger hovered by the trigger; weeks before, he killed another man in precisely this situation. Now, as the enemy raised his rifle, briefly meeting Leon's eyes—in that instant when any prey freezes— Leon still didn't fire. It wasn't a choice, not mercy, not foolishness: he simply didn't fire. He wondered where the enemy came from, if you could think there, and eat a meal in peace. He wondered why the enemy was the enemy.

Jackson thrashed in the brush behind, and the enemy, sensing perhaps an entire company, turned and ran.

Jackson emerged. "You okay?"

"Yes." Leon searched Jackson's eyes. "I—"

"You're gonna get us killed." Jackson stared down the trail. "Just . . . go on a little. We're there."

"Where?"

"Here. The CO says spend the night."

He slept well, dreamlessly, waking once to look up at the gigantic moon. At first light, weak but calm, he sat squeezing the boil. "Coffee," he murmured, remembering.

"No time," Jackson said. "We gotta go."

"Where?"

"Meet some birds." He lit a cigarette. "I'm tired, too, Leon. How you doin'?"

"I don't know."

"I believe that thing's gonna bust."

The boil had swollen overnight, and his face felt bloated, his neck stiff. Keeping his eyes on Jackson's boots, he made it to the field. The birds were delayed and Leon went off by himself, as though he would vomit. The others threw him sidelong glances, not quite in horror.

Leon knelt, pinched, and it rushed into his hands suddenly, a clot of yellowish goo and a dribble of blood. Poison, yet his chin resumed its strange old shape. He felt intensely sleepy. He sat in the dirt, lit a cigarette for something to do, and then the cigarette burned his fingers.

"You should go in," said Jackson, hovering like an angel. "Want me to talk to the lieutenant?"

"What you say?"

"You're sick, Leon. You should go in."

"I don't—" Here came the birds, so familiar they confused him. They might go in reverse, and he'd develop the boil again, freeze at sight of the enemy.

No! He was in the air again! In the cold air he expected to meet with his parents, with radiant Susan, but then he understood he was with the men. One of them shouted. What did he say?

"Short!" It was the door gunner, and "short" was an announcement, as for weddings and babies. "Short! Eight days!"

The gunner, Leon's acquaintance of dreams, was going home. He pulled iced Cokes from a canister, passed out crackers and smoked oysters: a party at three thousand feet. Leon liked oysters, but today, looking at them packed neatly in the tin, he almost retched. They were like his boil, his own putrid flesh. He closed his eyes to contain his nausea, and in the cold air, with the bird rocking, he thought of his father, who used to swing him in the back yard, high enough, almost, to touch the summer moon. Leon opened his eyes and saw the bird's shadow, spinning on the clouds below, then plummeting to the ground. They were coming down. "Where we going?"

The gunner shook his head. He adjusted his helmet and drew erect by the gun, took a swallow of Coke, spoke into the radio.

This time, Leon thought, this time. "Is it cold? Is it cold?"

The gunner lifted up the gun, cocked it. They dropped fast. Jackson nudged Leon's shoulder, grasped his forearm. "It's hot, Leon."

"Hot?"

"Hot."

"Hot?"

Every man tensed, arranged his gear, pushed his

feet out straight. The gunner began firing, aiming down at first, then locking his fire level into the wood line. The bird touched the grass, skimmed up a few inches, hovered.

"Out!" screamed Jackson. "Get the fuck out!"

"Oh God," said Leon. "Oh God oh God—"

The machine gun rattled. The others were off, running low for cover; the pilot turned, jerked his thumb angrily. The machine gun stopped. The gunner had slumped back, and bled below the chin.

"Leon, run!" Jackson screamed.

He did. *Blat blat blat blat* went the rotors, as the bird strained to rise, in the heavy air. Leon searched for Jackson, who could get him through.

"Leon, run!" But someone else had said it, because Jackson was dead. Leon rose, like a ghost out of his friend, and ran. He'd been here another time. He'd charged this same woods, done it again and again. Yet in the trees he saw what he hadn't before: one green shoulder behind a gun, like the corner of a dream, and the hint of a new world. Another man fell. Leon stood erect—-lightheaded, weary, sick—-and raised his rifle.

Called of God

WHEN THE HELICOPTER dropped him off he just stood there, a sick grin on his face. He seemed too frail to hold up all the gear they'd loaded him down with. It looked like he didn't know where he was and never would know, and I kept hoping he'd be assigned to second squad. I didn't want him on my conscience.

Naturally, Lieutenant Klein sent him to me. So I shook his hand and told him to drop his pack anywhere. Make some coffee, cock up his feet, stay a while.

"Yessir."

"What's your name?"

"Bobby Lee Daws."

"Well, Bobby Lee, this is the end of the line. You don't have to say 'sir' even to officers, and I sure as hell ain't no officer."

He nodded and plopped down in the dirt, his eyes held low. I gave him about two weeks. I patted him on the shoulder and said, "Just take it one thing at a time."

Then I grabbed my coffee and went up to see Klein.

Klein was smoking one of those little cigars and reading *Anna Karenina*. It was the longest book he could find. He'd been reading it for a month, all through the monsoon, and the glue dissolved. He'd peel off pages as he finished, throw them behind us as we moved through the brush— gingerbread crumbs. "Thanks a lot," I said.

The lieutenant studied his cigar. "He's what they sent, Irish. Quality control ain't my MOS. Put him on point."

They called me Irish because in the mornings, to get going, I'd pour a little whiskey in my coffee. I'd do it in the evenings, too, to get stopped. "I don't know about the point, Butch. Man gets killed, it's right away. If we was to kinda watch over him for a while—"

"Shit," Klein said, flipping the cigar down into his foxhole, reaching for another. "If he's any good, he'll make it. Put him out there, Irish. Baptism in fire."

When we took a break or camped for the night Bobby Lee read the Bible, holding it close to his face in the fading light. On guard I heard him whispering prayers. "You a preacher?" I asked.

"I been waitin' for the call." He said it like it settled everything.

"What's that?"

"The Lord tells you, Irish . . . what you have to do."

"Huh. In a dream, like?"

"It can happen in a dream, but most times you hear this voice."

"And this voice, it tells you to be president of the United States or something?"

"Even a garbage man."

"Well, I don't think I'd listen, Bobby Lee, if some voice told me to be a garbage man. You ought to aim for truck driver, at least."

He didn't smile. "Whether it's humble or mighty," he said sternly, "the Bible tells us to do what the Lord wills."

"Fuckin' A," I said. Why not? It didn't matter to me if he was in love with an elephant. The great surprise was that he'd become a good point man. Maybe it was because he was a country boy—at home in the woods, cautious, alert in exactly the right way. Anyhow, six weeks of prayer and Bible readings went by. Nothing much happened, and Bobby Lee began to seem like good luck.

I was walking second in thick brush. I got hung up in some vines, and by the time I could work myself loose Bobby Lee might have been fifty feet ahead. Nothing lonelier on earth than for him to turn around then, and see that I wasn't there. It was like somebody wrote the script. I heard two rifles firing, and a scream.

We hit the ground. I eased off my pack, thumbed my rifle to automatic, and crawled forward on my knees. But it was the other man who was dead. Bobby Lee stood looking out into the woods,weaving slightly, like he was going to be sick. "Hey, man," I said.

The dead man was an officer. You could tell because the officers always wore Browning nine-millimeter pistols or one of those worthless Russian watches. Sometimes you could trade the pistols, which were Belgian-made and pretty, for a rear job. But this guy had a watch. Karl Marx should have been on the dial, jerking his arms around.

Bobby Lee sat on the ground, digging in the sand with a stick. I meant to cheer him up. "You got an officer, man! Headed him off at the pass!"

He stared like he thought I was the devil himself. "I won't do that no more, Irish."

Klein poked his head through the leaves. "Real fine, real fine," he said, glancing over the scene. "An officer! Let me see that watch, Irish."

Sometimes a man got a kill and turned cocky. He grew more dangerous to himself and everyone around him than if he'd just stepped off the plane. But I figured Bobby Lee was too meek to come down with blood-lust. He'd had his baptism in fire. I could stop worrying about him.

I thought there was just the right balance in him, of caution and fearlessness, to make him the best man I had. When his turn to point came around again I was eating crackers and cheese, sipping my coffee, and thinking soon I'd be home. Garcia came back along the file. "Irish. You know Bobby Lee, he don't have his gun."

"Huh?"

"He won't pick it up."

"No rifle?"

"That's what I fucking *said,* man." Garcia shrugged elaborately.

I stopped the platoon and grabbed the unclaimed rifle as I moved up toward the point team. Bobby Lee sat on his pack. "Here's your weapon, Mister."

"I don't want it."

"You think . . . your heavenly father will protect you?" Then I remembered. "Oh shit. Did you get the call, Bobby Lee?"

He didn't answer, and I tried again. "Listen, man: easy day. Half a click to go—then we'll talk about it, OK? C'mon, let's go."

He shook his head. "It's the Lord's will, Irish. The Bible says, 'Thou shalt not kill.' It don't say you can kill in a war or somethin'."

"Bobby Lee, you ignorant fucker! Listen, this is serious. This is—"

Klein buzzed me on the radio. "What's going on up there? You guys jacking off?"

The men sprawled out with cigarettes and cans of fruit. I had a headache: too much coffee, not enough crackers and cheese. Klein arrived, cigarless, *Anna Karenina* poking out of his side pocket. "Problem?"

"Bobby Lee won't carry his rifle."

"Too heavy? Poor baby, he's tired."

"Doesn't want to kill anybody, he says."

"Well, I don't, either. Too fucking hot. I want

to get set up for the night and read my book. That it? You overheated, Bobby Lee?"

"That's it," I said. "He's hot. Let me point into camp, Lieutenant. I don't mind."

Bobby Lee lifted his chin. "Nosir, I'm fine. I just ain't carryin' no gun. I killed one man, and I been prayin' it through, and the Lord, He *said* to me—"

"He got the call," I explained.

"The what?"

"The call."

"Ah," Klein murmured. He shook his head slowly. "Sergeant York."

"Who's that?"

"This Tennessee hillbilly, real religious, back in the First World War. Saw a light . . . decided he was a conscientious objector. Bobby Lee—"

"Gary Cooper?" I asked.

"Right. Bobby Lee, listen. Go ahead and point, no weapon, it's your life. We hit the shit, you'll be an ever-lovin' martyr. What is it, special place in Heaven? Or are you just shamming it? You're scared, troop, and you think this bullshit will get you home. Well, I'm here to tell you, Bobby Lee: that will not happen."

"I never said I wouldn't point, sir," Bobby Lee said. He rose and shouldered his pack. "I ain't tryin' to get out of nothin'." He began moving forward.

"Lieutenant—" I began.

"Let him go, Irish."

"Butch, I tell you, he's serious. What if he walks into an ambush?"

"He won't last that long. You watch, he'll *beg* for that rifle. I give him five minutes."

It was like some guy in a wheelchair was our first line of defense. It was worse because you could tell that Bobby Lee was no Daniel: He was scared, and kept mumbling. His fear drifted back and settled on every man's face. Maybe it was God's will that Klein didn't push very hard; we hadn't gone two hundred meters before he signaled to make camp.

"The thing about Sergeant York," Klein said, "is that when it got rough, when he saw his buddies getting shot, he picked up his weapon and blew the fucking Huns away."

"Bobby Lee never heard of Sergeant York. Maybe not even of Gary Cooper."

"What am I supposed to do? This could ruin my career, Irish." It was dark by then. Around the camp, as if from a signal, every tiny noise ceased. Klein drew on his cigar.

"Better cup that light, Butch."

"Yeah. What's wrong with me, Irish?"

"Nothing's wrong. You just get to thinking you're a real person sometimes, instead of an officer."

"Well, fuck you. Listen, why can't he act like everybody else? This is no tight ship. I don't want to come down on him."

"He's weird. Send him in."

"How's it gonna look? Lieutenant Ronald Klein turns soldiers into COs."

"Say he's nuts. I mean . . . isn't he?"

It seemed like a good idea to me, but at first light Klein strode over, looking grim, and shoved his face near Bobby Lee's. "You *will* carry that weapon."

Bobby Lee looked like he'd cry. "Nosir."

"Nosir! We're not talking about a goddamn slap on the hands here, soldier. We're talking court-martial. You think that'll get you back to the World? Not exactly. Long Binh Jail, troop. L. B. fucking J. Let me tell you, let me give you a little inkling, what it's like. You go to the first line, you come to attention, you salute. You say, 'Permission to use the latrine, sir.' You go to the next line. 'Permission to use the latrine, sir.' You get the idea, Bobby Lee? How fucking copy?"

"Solid copy, sir." His head bowed low. "But I *cain't*. I cain't carry no gun. I would go to hell."

"On your feet!"

He rose. We all were watching; we all had been in the same situation, where an officer, your friend, was suddenly an officer again, grinding you into the dirt. Yet it would have been over some prostitute or drinking on duty, not refusing to carry your weapon. Klein thrust the rifle forward, released it as Bobby Lee's arms rose involuntarily. The rifle fell to the sand. Shock waves went out into the jungle. Sacrilege.

"Sergeant!"

"Yessir!" I said.

"This man will point today."

"Yessir."

"I want you to take his water."

"Sir—"

The lieutenant glared.

"Yessir."

No air moved, and the trees themselves seemed to sweat. The far distance seemed murky and feverish, indistinguishable from the oily, distorted sun. Bobby Lee reached around for the canteen that wasn't there. He fell, rose, and looked toward me like he didn't know what he'd done wrong. I pointed toward Garcia, who carried the disputed rifle. Bobby Lee set his jaw, and rushed forward, but a vine caught him. He spun violently, only to grow more entwined. I glanced back. Klein watched, smoking his little cigar; he murmured something to the second squad leader.

Garcia cut away the vines. Bobby Lee kept jerking; his helmet fell off and his hair looked like a wet mop. "Go easy," Garcia told him.

"I love the Lord!"

"Hey, hey, man," said Garcia. "This lieutenant is crazy. You ought to do it, a little thing. Take the weapon. You fall down, I know, he'll say, 'Piss on that soldier.' Every*one*, we with you, man. You're *right*. But hey, man, he'll kill you. You'll die."

Yet Bobby Lee burst away, running almost one hundred meters. Then, in an open area, he staggered and plopped down in the grass.

"What's this?" said Klein, suddenly beside me. "He stopped in the open?"

"Give him a drink," Garcia said.

"I think we ought to, sir. Give him a drink." I'd said "sir," and Klein dropped his eyes to me and stared, like he felt betrayed. "You miss the point, Irish."

"I don't miss the point, sir, but it won't work. He's too ignorant. Pretty soon he'll stroke out, and we'll have to Medevac him. Send him back with the mail, sir."

Klein shook his head and hurried across the clearing. "Ready for a drink, Bobby Lee?"

His eyes were red and far away. He'd gone pale, except for where the vines scraped his face and the blood puckered. He nodded.

"Garcia has your weapon, Bobby Lee. Pick it up, you don't have to point. Ever. You can carry ammo."

"Nosir."

"Nosir! You want to risk every man? My God! Then point, point! On your feet!"

Bobby Lee stood and tried a few more steps into the woods again, but in moments he slumped against a tree. His head flopped, and his body went slack and gray. He seemed pinned to the wood.

The medic pressed salt water to his lips, but Bobby Lee turned his head. "Drink, fuckhead!" said the medic, and Bobby Lee drank again and again, as though brine were spring water. At last he smiled and his breathing slowed. No anger whatever now. He stared off with a kind of fool's peace.

"On your feet!" said Klein.

"Lieutenant—" I began.

"Shut up! Soldier, on your feet!"

Bobby Lee tried to rise, but couldn't. Klein knelt before him, shouting into his face. "We're leaving you here, you understand? Leaving you for Charley. Unless you take your weapon . . . *here!*" Klein shoved out the rifle. At first Bobby Lee seemed not to recognize it. Then he raised his hand and batted the stock away.

Klein never faltered. He stood, shouldered his gear, and began walking. "Move out!"

He would not have abandoned Bobby Lee. He couldn't have gotten away with it: *he'd* have been the one requesting permission to piss. It must have been his final test, to see if Bobby Lee would pick up the rifle and follow. Wouldn't he? Wouldn't anyone, left to die? Or would Bobby Lee have passed on into the exquisite pain of martyrs?

"No way!" Garcia screamed. "No *way*, Lieutenant!"

"No?" said Klein. "Garcia . . . no?" He looked at me, amazement on his face. "Irish? You? No?"

"No, Butch," I said.

"No!" Garcia threw his rifle down. Behind him was a clatter, curses, as a dozen more threw down their rifles, too.

So—in the open place—we called for resupply. We read our mail and ate cookies from our aunts and maybe changed shirts. I had some whiskey. The sun dropped low, and Klein smoked cigars and sat staring at the last pages of *Anna Karenina*.

Garcia and I helped Bobby Lee onto the helicopter. Though I made a point of asking, I never heard of him again. Except for his one craziness, there was nothing special about him. You might have hoped he went from outfit to outfit, like a sort of Johnny Appleseed, refusing to carry rifles. More likely, he spent his last ten months on KP.

As we began to move out again, I had the notion not to pick up my rifle. Just for a moment, and then I grabbed it as always. I had only a month to go and didn't want to make any trouble, and when you come right down to it, I was never all that religious.

Human Wave

Nolan's company arrived just at dawn, in a blinding whirl—and then collapsed on the high dune. Fanned by sea breezes, Nolan slept.

Around 1000 a rumor went up and down the squads that they were about to attack the enemy's flank, but no one stirred. They were a burial detail, picking up after Bravo Company. All that remained of the enemy was their stench.

At 1400 they divided into files on either side the road, and marched toward the smoldering firebase. Topping another dune, they could see the island more clearly, with its temple rising high, and the Buddha staring down upon the brown sea. Near the mainland, some Australians were surfing.

Surfing, Nolan thought. *Surfing*.

Directly ahead, men searched the scrub palms. Holding handkerchiefs to their faces, they dragged the dead out and dropped them—for slow review as you passed. The dead were covered with sand, and ants, and they'd turned black.

Nolan had never seen a dead man, other than his grandfather at the funeral. He'd been in-country precisely seventeen days. He was proud he didn't retch.

They entered the battlefield, where bodies were piled high, and Hennessey, new as he, drew near. "I heard they was just gonna pour diesel fuel on 'em, like you burn shit?" He focused his camera over the shoulder of the man ahead of him, and upon all the men in line, descending toward the ruined firebase. He whirled and aimed at Nolan. "Only then the TV people flew in."

Nolan tried to smile and yet keep moving, keep his rifle swinging. Who could say where Hennesey's photo would find a home? "Why *not* burn them? If you're dead, what's the difference?"

"It was barbaric, man!" The camera whirred just as Nolan blinked. "You cain't put a thing like that on the evenin' news. So they flew in the dozers to dig trenches—nothin' to it in the sand." Hennessey seemed puzzled. "That *seems* better, don't you think?"

"The bodies—"

"Some of 'em been there a week now. I guess the gooks try to drag 'em off at night. Jeez, they gotta be ripe."

Small arms broke out. Everyone hit the sand; down in the salty grass, Nolan lost his sense of where Hennessey was. He was afraid to call out. Once before this had happened, and he'd pissed his pants, but was so soaked in sweat already it didn't make much difference.

Now he saw that others rose, that some men had never dropped. Hennessey inspected his camera for grit, and Nolan, trying to project calm, reached for a canteen. A second lieutenant came trotting down the road. "Fuckin' cherry," he said, and Nolan turned in alarm, but the lieutenant winked. "Fuckin' cherry. Shootin' at a dead man!"

Human wave! Hundreds of men—but who, what mind, could be alien enough to charge into machine guns? Nolan imagined savage hordes, scimitars raised, their very souls crazed with opium.

Bodies lay in black clumps like a meteor had dropped from the sky, burst into flaming pieces, and scorched the grass as it cooled. Nolan kicked at a clump, and discovered the blackness wasn't from fire. He leapt back from the flies—rising in a high whine, settling like a blanket.

Something rustled in the thicket to his right.

A wounded man, he thought, crouching. To the query in Hennessey's eyes Nolan shook his head, and brought a finger to his lips. As Hennessey raised his camera, Nolan crawled forward, digging his rifle stock into the sand like a real soldier. He parted the brush.

A huge black man, naked, sat on a tattered parachute; a woman slept beside him. The man clasped his hands in an attitude of prayer, and rocked forward, eyes closed. Down his ribcage were moist red splotches of jungle rot, garish, unconvincing, like the makeup in a horror movie. The man didn't acknowledge Nolan, but suddenly the woman opened her eyes.

"Excuse me," Nolan said.

"Scuse?"

Nolan backed away, his eyes locked on the black man, who still meditated. He stood and brushed at the sand.

"Dead or alive?" asked Hennessey.

He didn't know how to answer. He began walking again, like an explorer entering upon some great natural wonder. The drifting smoke, the bulldozers grunting down by the sea, that charred helicopter, the endless confusion of wire twisting around the firebase—all seemed to whirl.

A little flatbed truck pulled near, loaded with dead; flies clung like paint. The driver was masked, his dull gray snout hanging like a baboon's nostrils. Sweat streamed out of his hair and his forehead had erupted in a rash. The man raised a hand, and Nolan nodded hello. Was the moon man smiling? Someone prayed in the bushes. Someone grinned as he chauffeured the dead?

Hennessey, who'd captured a nice panorama of the the gleaming ocean, the island picturesque between the dunes, framed Nolan before the truck load of dead. "Smile."

"No. Don't, man—"

"Your old lady'll love it. Smile." The camera whirred.

"You're crazy!" said Nolan. "You think I, you think I could—what's wrong?"

Hennessey's face was white, and wrenched. He jabbed his finger at the truck, but it was everywhere, like tear gas, like you'd been breathing through a tube and someone pinched it off.

Nolan's lungs heaved. Every man picked up his feet. Oh, run!

"I'm really a pacifist," Nolan said, his words drifting out before him for study, like smoke rings. He was stoned, hard to say on what. He'd been talking to a soldier who didn't reply, but simply sat on the opposite bunk and strummed a guitar, in the dim light, as though Nolan wasn't there. A dozen men had crowded into the bunker, but when the rain stopped they all went off with Hennessey, laughing, speaking foreign tongues.

"I mean, I almost went to Canada." The silent soldier gave a little flamenco flourish, as if to underscore Nolan's stand for peace. "But I thought, I'd never see my parents again, or my girl. Do you have a girl?"

Nolan held out a photo, its edges curled from moisture, of his true love. The soldier kissed it like a cross. Then a grenade rolled across the floor.

There were raindrops on it, and it sparkled. Staring, Nolan realized that in seconds he'd die. One, two, three, he counted, calmly, then leaped from the bunk, and lay jerking spasmodically. Four, five, six, he thought, staring up at the filament in the light bulb.

The soldier kept playing his guitar. "That's just Fast Man. Screws out the blasting cap, screws the top back on, pulls the ring. He's *so* funny."

And here he was, beckoning—the prayerful black man Nolan had met in the thicket. His eyes fled helplessly to the man's rotting skin, and he couldn't speak. He followed meekly to the roof of the bunker, where there was a sort of chaise longue made of sand bags and flak jackets, all of it wet. Wordlessly, Nolan slid behind the machine gun.

"When they lights up the sky, Nolan, you shoot this mother."

"You know my name?"

Fast Man laughed. "I am Pie-in-the-Sky. I knows you like the back of my ass. I am your C of fucking O, cherry boy, Nolan babes."

"You're an officer? Sir?"

"I surely am, and this here is your on-the-job training. Are we ready on the right, are we ready on the left?" He lowered his voice, as if calling from a distance. "We is *ready* on the right, we is *ready* on the left. Aim that sucker!"

"There's nothing out there!"

But flares popped, lending the damp night luminescence. "You shoot at the rats, white boy. If you don't see no ghosts."

"Ghosts? You mean the gooks? Come back for their buddies?"

"Fire!" said Fast Man, and the perimeter opened up, under the quaking light. Someone detonated a barrel of fougas and a tower of red flame rose, crisscrossed with green tracers— Nolan's own. He got under a rat and lifted it up into the concertina, where it hung until the gunner from the next bunker joined in, and cut it in two. "Fine," said Fast Man. "You good."

"I had an expert rating in Basic."

"No shit? Well, drive on, Expert. See them ghosts?"

He did. Nolan swore he saw them, men rising, men dancing, as round after round sank into the mass of bodies. The ghosts seemed to be brandishing rifles. He opened up.

"You really good," said Fast Man.

Nolan fired and fired again, hardly conscious of Fast Man bending near, to fasten new clips. It was marvelous how the shadows danced. He knew he hit them because of the lovely green tracers.

"Ceasefire!" Fast Man yelled.

"Wow," said Nolan, leaning back in the chaise longue.

"You all right, Nolan," Fast Man said. "We gonna work you right into the program."

Nolan sat in the mess tent, nose pointed into the sea breeze. Men bustled everywhere around him, with a sense of purpose in the morning's restorative air.

He drank three cups of coffee and gulped aspirin but something hung on from the night, a sort of after-image when he moved his head quickly. An hour passed. The heat bore down, the wind shifted, and he smelled the bodies again. Officers eyed him suspiciously, and he brought out a tablet to write to his girl.

Two other men also waited, but they didn't speak to him even when he asked, "You guys waiting for Fast Man?" They talked in whispers, with intimate nods and murmurs, inexplicable, quick laughter. One had a nasty cut up his cheek, bruised-looking along the stitches.

"Nolan, my man!"

Nolan felt relief, and a flood of trust, in seeing Fast Man again, yet his eyes leaped helplessly to the camera hanging around Fast Man's neck. Fast Man's grin changed to an expression of sympathy. "That man was your friend. Babes, I'm sorry! He went out in the night."

"Hennessey? Was he hit?"

"One of them ghosts blowed away his kneecap. Million dollar wound. *Lucky* . . . dudes was linin' up to shake that man's hand. " Fast Man grinned again. "Big bird come in, carried that man *away.*"

Nolan glanced at the two men, who stood now, and nodded. "But his camera—"

"Been needin' a good camera. 'Let me buy that from you, Mr. Million Dollars,' I told him. 'You be in Japan, they got everything you need there, dirt cheap.' Ever been to Japan, babes?"

"Fast Man . . . I mean, *wow.* You know how I can write him? We went through Basic together."

"Sure, babes. Come over to my house sometime, we set you up. Fast Man never let you down, Nolan. Now. Look here. Time to go to work, babes."

The two men crept near.

"This is your team, Nolan. This is Lewis—" Fast Man nodded to the man with the cut. Nolan offered his hand, but Lewis drew back, and merely smiled.

"And this man is Sergeant Fisher."

Fisher saluted with one finger.

"Now these men are good men, Nolan. They know the score here in this combat area. You are in good hands with these men. Ain't no jiveassin' with these men."

"Fast Man. Sir. Hennessey's old lady gave him that camera. I just don't understand—"

"New man, naturally, he gonna worry some," Fast Man said. "But you gonna be *fine*, Nolan babes, if you do what your team members say to do. I got faith in you. Ain't no jiveassin' with a man like you. Keep your shit straight, do a good job for Fast Man, your team members gonna find you a woman. Hey." Fast Man grinned, and slapped Nolan's back. "Like that, wouldn't you, babes?"

Fisher motioned to the pickup bed, but before Nolan found a grip the sergeant popped the clutch and roared onto the road. He veered off across the smoky plain, and shifted to high when they reached the beach. They passed the Australians, out surfing in the shallow waters that reached to the little island. A big, yellow-haired man flexed his biceps, and waved.

Fisher hit the brakes, and turned the truck into a skid. Nolan nearly fell off the side. As he regained his balance, Fisher slammed into reverse and spun backward into a stand of scrub palms. He cut the engine. He opened the door but continued to sit, rolling a joint. Nolan came slowly around as Fisher struck a match on the dash. "Where you from in the World, Cherry Boy?"

"Ohio. Van Wert, Ohio." Nolan stared at the joint, which Fisher passed to Lewis. Lewis walked to the front of the truck, where he smoked and looked out toward the island. He pulled a Frisbee from under his shirt and tossed it gently from hand to hand.

"They got any women in Van Wert?" Fisher asked. "I mean, Lewis and I were discussing it, you look queer to us."

Nolan took a step backward, bumping into Lewis. Lewis grinned and ran a finger along his cut, and pulled out one of his stitches.

"You guys are crazy," Nolan said.

"He thinks we're crazy," Lewis said, returning the joint to Fisher.

"Everybody *here* is crazy," Nolan said. "God, I wish I'd gone to Canada. I don't belong here." He sighed. "You guys aren't really like this, are you? You're just giving me shit."

"Oh, yes." Fisher smiled and released smoke. "We're plumb loco, no question about it. How it is, Cherry Boy, me and Lewis been under a strain. We been traumatized. We'll have to live with this for years in our civilian lives."

"Tell you one thing," said Lewis. He jabbed Fisher's ribs and grinned. All he did was grin. "We're not crazy enough to load them stinking gooks on the truck."

He hadn't smelled them because the wind blew toward the sea, but he saw them now, maybe twenty in a great pile. "I gotta do it by myself?"

"'Fraid so," Fisher said. "How it is, see, me and

Lewis got ourselves a union. We just drive. We're going up the beach now, and play with the girls, while you *load*." He stretched out his hand to Lewis, who'd kept the joint too long. Lewis kept sucking, and Fisher shoved him. "You get done, come see us."

"Got to work before you play," Lewis said, at last returning the joint. He began rolling another.

Nolan followed them for a few steps. "I refuse to do this alone!"

"Please," said Lewis.

"Do it for the team," said Fisher.

They went a distance down the beach, men the same height, walking almost in step. They turned in unison.

"Masks are in the cab," Fisher called.

"Real man don't need no mask," said Lewis. He lit the new joint while Fisher took off his boots and walked along in the water. The two nodded, and laughed, almost simultaneously. Lewis pulled out his Frisbee and Fisher ran ahead, leaped high and gracefully, caught it.

Nolan sat on the tailgate, with the sea lapping quietly in. He watched the fisherman pulling in their nets, and returning to the island.

He found Lewis and Fisher's stash and rolled himself a joint, then sat leafing through *Playboy*. He tried donning a mask, couldn't secure it, tossed it aside. He rocked back and forth with the rhythm of the waves, then suddenly jerked to his feet and stumbled into the palms.

He dragged a body back by its heels. Ants issued from its mouth, and somehow an orange slime appeared on his shirt. He was surprised how little the body weighed.

He shoved it into the bed, and judged that he could get through this, when his breakfast rose. He ran to the water and vomited. He looked up at last, blearily, his chest heaving. He could almost make out the features of the men on the island, working methodically under the Buddha's eye. "Fast Man, you prick," he murmured.

Down the beach fifty meters the yellow-haired Australian did calisthenics. He had beautiful muscles. Maybe he was Mr. Australia. He waved, and nodded in sympathy. "Ain't it the shits, mate?"

"It's insane," Nolan said. "God Almighty, it's, it's—"

"It's the shits, mate."

Nolan stood weakly, and shuffled toward the palms. He smoked another joint by the pickup door. Far up the beach, Lewis and Fisher threw their Frisbee. The girls, driving little motor scooters, began arriving. Okay, Nolan thought, an initiation. I can do this.

The dead men were hardly distinguishable, flowing together like cheese shrunken in the sun.

But here, this one, take him: the side of his face, though waxen and greenish, seemed human, still. Nolan turned him over, and the leathery flesh tore away . . . his hands crawled with maggots. Suddenly, his arms and chest were covered with slick, gleaming things. He swept at them frantically, stamped the sand, and backed away, gagging in the violated air.

The team had gone out of sight. Even the Australian had vanished. No, there he was, a few feet into the surf, snorkeling.

And another four on the truck, by their boots. Easier by the boots. Oh yes, he could do this. He was a pacifist, but could do this . . . and afterwards he'd drink a cold Coke, and smoke another joint, and maybe go off into the weeds with a prostitute. He'd be loco enough by then.

He tried not to look. He tried to send another self ahead to do the dirty work. He tried to hover above it all. But now, when he pulled out yet another leg, and the bruised face rolled over, he saw Hennessey.

Of course not. If so, the man certainly had some explaining to do. Hennessey was in Japan. He'd been shot while playing Frisbee. With the same presence with which he'd counted off Fast Man's dud grenade, Nolan saw that a trip wire was tied to the dead man's neck, and stretched to his hand. Because he'd turned the body over, Nolan had yanked the pin from the grenade.

As he counted, three, four, Nolan wondered how the Australian knew. He ran toward the truck. "Mate! Mate!" he cried. "Booby trap!" Boobies were some sort of bird, weren't they? A trap for booby birds. Very funny. Nolan threw his hands before his face, and leaped back.

The moon hung low over the sea, impossibly

large and red. He'd been lying among the dead, and quickly, horrified, he rose and ran down the beach. He knelt to wash his face and hands. They had abandoned him!

He was angry, yet afraid. Lunatics. Lunatics everywhere around him. Lightheaded, thirsty, cold, he walked toward the brightly-lit firebase. Stumbling into the dead, he ran toward the light— any light; a flare popped directly above him. He stood by still more dead men, who pulled up together as if from the soil. More flares, and he waved his rifle frantically, jumped up and down, and shouted.

He heard the faint call: "Fire!"

The night transformed into flame. Bullets dug up the sand around him, and strafed the dead men. They thought he was a gook! He dropped to the sand, writhed, curled in among the dead.

"Follow me, Nolan."

A huge black man, his chest gleaming with wounds, stood in the half-light by the sea.

"Fast Man, is it you? This is a mistake. I—"

The flares winked out. "Ceasefire!" echoed faintly. Nolan ran along the beach, following the wounded black man, and called, "Fast Man!" No one answered. He heard no sound but the water, and a subtle rustling, like wind, as dark men came in waves off the field, and entered the water.

Again he heard his name, and seemed to see Fast Man's head, rolling over and over.

He imagined this. He was in the middle of a dream and would awaken in Japan, in a hospital, screaming. Yet still he entered the water, and swam toward the island, the dim, yellow Buddha. Salt burned at the hole in his stomach, but he found he could swim almost effortlessly.

The New Captain

BY THE TIME the old captain was finished a third of us were wounded or dead, and the rest had been pushed so hard for so long that we were all nerves and suspicions, reduced to feeding our faces and hoping for one night's uninterrupted sleep. We went forty-three days without a hot meal or bath, until no one's skin was quite black or white or brown, but the green of mold, and scum. Then, like a period of mourning, the old captain was gone, and we stood in formation at Tay Ninh, saying goodbye. He saluted the colonel and the new captain, saluted us, and without a word stalked up the hill, toward a jeep piled with gear. He was a major now, en route to Germany.

The new captain put us at parade rest and delivered his admonishments: there would be no drug use, and no one would be allowed to get the clap. Captain John Sorley was not, however, a Billy Bad Ass. He respected us. Frankly, he was here because of his faith in America and in the American infantry, the finest fighting force in the world. He'd volunteered for active duty and for combat because he was sick of what was going on back home. Even his guard unit was filled with malcontents.

Standard stuff, though usually we heard still more admonishments, and somewhat less patriotism. Of course, patriots weren't rare—about as common as Christians. This one was plump and pushing forty: too old, you'd have thought, for war.

But, at twenty-four, so was I.

I was an acting platoon sergeant—lieutenants kept getting killed right and left of me. Were it a movie I would have been the quiet one, the veteran who seldom showed his emotions but was, under fire, cool and dependable. Not exactly, but none of the men I'd come in-country with were around to dispute my image. The truth was more nearly that my anger had so burned itself out that I hadn't anything left to say. What made me go was a desire to return home that ran so deep you might have called it delirium.

Sorley was my fourth captain; I could hardly respond when he came around, next day, to introduce himself. "How are you, Jonesy?'

"Fine, sir. It's Jones, not Jonesy."

"I thought everybody called you Jonesy."

"Yes, sir." I shrugged. "They do."

"Forty days to go?"

"Thirty-nine, sir."

"Man like you," he mumbled. He stuck out a hand and then stood too near, so that I could smell his breath. It was sweet—and alcoholic. "Time to re-up!"

"I guess not, sir. I've made it this far—"

"You've done your duty." A change rippled over his face, and he stepped into the movies. "Where you from, son?"

"Arkansas."

He grunted. I should have been from Brooklyn or maybe West Texas, which would have bagged and tagged me. Apparently, there was nothing to say about Arkansas. "Fine state," he muttered, and moved on.

Late the following day two things happened: it began to rain, and my platoon received an order to fly out to an utterly forsaken rice paddy. We were to set up an ambush. This last was bad enough, but in the rain it would be miserable. It was an odd assignment, out of the blue, and I wondered if Sorley had volunteered us.

Anyhow here he was, with bandoliers across his chest, and grenades strung from his ears, motioning impatiently toward the chopper pad down the hill a quarter mile. "C'mon, men!" he shouted, and began to run. No birds were in sight, so I didn't run after him, and neither did the men. He turned, a little anger, and a lot of disappointment, on his face, and I guess it was the disappointment that made us pick up our feet. No need to hurt his feelings. We reached the pad, stood around smoking cigarettes and getting wet, until the birds bore down over the hill.

A foot of water covered the paddy. The pilots hovered two feet above it, while we slid down into the mud. Sorley led us to high ground, by a stand of denuded wild oranges. No one has been here since the French, I thought. It was almost dark, and raining so hard you wondered how you had space to breathe.

We made a poor camp—simply snapping together our ponchos for hooches, and crawling under. It was too dark and wet to cook—I had a can of ham slices, and some soda crackers. The ground was sodden. When at last a stream rolled into the hooch, we got up and dug a ditch. After that, life was tolerable. I rolled myself in my poncho liner like a cigar, and chain-smoked.

Toward midnight the rain stopped and the stars popped out, but there was a cold wind. I slept a while and then woke from horrible dreams: news my mother was dead, or the discovery I had no legs. Sometime before the dawn I heard a terrible crashing in the brush—grabbed my rifle, nearly fired. Could somebody be out there? *Here?*

Of course, it was Sorley, excited, out of breath. "Jonesy!" he whispered.

"Yessir."

"We've got a man on the moon!"

"What?"

"It came over the radio. Right now! An American on the moon!"

"No shit, sir."

"Pass it on."

"Yessir."

I went back to sleep. In woods like these, I could have dreamed it all, awake or sleeping. Next morning, though, as we waited for the birds to return us for breakfast, I glanced at Sorley and thought, this one bears watching.

I had thirty-one days left when they dropped the company by a broad, nameless river, along which stretched forty miles and more of bamboo. No activity was reported, though six months before a battalion chased the enemy up and down the shore. Or maybe it was the other way around, but either way, lots of men died.

It was beautiful country, to be so full of ghosts. The river ran quietly, a resolute traveling companion; and the bamboo, never bombed, was virgin, mammoth. Clumps of it had trunks eight and ten inches in diameter, a slick, wet green that rose branchless for twenty feet, then sealed off the sky. The ground was even, with a deep layer of packed dry leaves. Worms worked in the rich, dark soil.

Sorley didn't move us far in a day, so we had time to secure our hooches before the rain, and then to play casino, or chess—and write letters, and dream. Suddenly, I had twenty-six days left, and my men, certain I'd make it, regarded me almost with reverence.

Sometimes, we came upon evidence of battle: a circle of foxholes, and a bunker complex that had served as a hospital. There were broken cots, mildewed bandages, decayed riggings for traction. The bamboo was splintered and brown here, with the sky poking through, and deer browsing in the ruins.

As each site Sorley fanned us in a circle and insisted on examining every shell casing and hooch pole. The time passed regardless. None of these ghosts could shoot.

He'd stride off inside the perimeter with Lieutenant Mason in tow, nodding, expostulating; he'd whirl suddenly, and point; he'd kneel, trace the leaves with troop movements and strategies. Often we made camp early, and Sorley sent out patrols the remainder of the day. Not at all in character for commanders, Sorley often led them himself, even taking the point sometimes—with his eyes narrowed and his jaw set. It was meaningless, but that was no innovation.

Things were fine until the day my platoon drew the point, and Screwy Louie found the snake. It was a python thick as a flagpole and twelve feet long, draped over the crotches of three clumps of bamboo. It was sluggish. Sorley came forward and stared for the longest time, but he hadn't a word. There was no point in disturbing the thing, but abruptly—in his idea of impressing the new captain or in veteran lunacy—Louie leaped forward with his machete, and hacked behind the snake's head. It lashed about, busting up bamboo. Two others joined Louie with their own machetes, but the snake was tough, mostly bone, and moving besides, so that it took several minutes to sever its head. The thing came to ground somehow and went on thrashing. Sorley stumbled back, his grin plastered over nausea. The company moved quickly, gratefully past.

And now the bamboo closed in. We had maps, every hour we calculated coordinates, but still we were lost. Your eyes couldn't penetrate the green for more than a hundred feet, and what you did see was clump after clump of bamboo, each clump identical. The branches arched above to form tunnels that burrowed off in a dozen directions, and I realized that I hadn't seen the sky for a week. Late every day, rain fell on the mat above us as on a roof, then dripped through, down your back, into your stinging eyes. The men trudged like the gray figures of a dream, seldom speaking and then only in whispers, their duties so deeply routine they went about them like zombies.

Night was worse. There might have been deer and monkeys, birds and buffalo, but you couldn't hear them: only the mumbling river, and the bamboo. No other sound like bamboo: creaking, chafing and moaning, shrieking with the rise of wind. Perhaps the moon shone oblong on the water, or hung distorted in the forlorn sky, and the bamboo took on the sound of men talking— zombies in the high branches, arguing in Vietnamese. I thought of my grandfather, lungs nearly finished from emphysema, out on his front porch rocking on the pine floor, creaking . . . and then, with an effort, I shut everything out, and slept. No one was there.

Then I woke, the wind had ceased, and the leaves throbbed with moonlight; above the river's dull roar I heard only silence. The bamboo creaked again, just once. Oh, it doesn't matter, I told myself, and sat awake until the dawn, my thoughts merged with the river, floating away like a dream.

It was on such a night, fifteen days down the river, when Sorley's nightmares began. "Oh . . . " moaned the captain. And then he shouted it: "Granville! Is that you?" I rose, and with Lieutenant Mason stumbled toward his position.

"Sir. Sir," the lieutenant hissed. "Please. No."

"I'm sorry," the captain said.

It went on for the next several nights, in the silences before dawn. I'd slip over with Mason and the medic, and hold Sorley by his shoulders. "Don't tell anybody about this, Jonesy," he said. Sometimes he screamed like a wounded man, and you wanted to shoot him full of morphine. "Shh. Hush, sir. Not here," the lieutenant told him, in a hoarse whisper.

"Did I do it again?"

"We *have* to be quiet, sir."

"A dream. I'm all right now. My uncle, his name was Granville—"

"Granville, sir," I said. "Hush."

"He only had one arm. He used to try to hug me, and it scared me, when I was a kid."

"In the morning, sir," said Mason.

What the medic gave him helped, but still in the daytime Sorley's face swelled as if from a sting, and his eyes, which seemed tiny and deep, were bloodshot. You could see him laboring to hide a kind of guilt, reaching out to any man who looked at him for understanding—patience, forgiveness. The men avoided his eyes. They'd ceased to believe in him.

There was nothing in these woods, we told him. Bamboo was like that: full of spooks. He said he knew it, that he'd briefly lost his confidence, lost his bearings. He called me Jonesy but seemed, as the sedative overtook him, to confuse me with his son. His son was in college, and a draft resister. How was it, Sorley lamented, that a man who had belonged to the union, who had served in the guard for seventeen years, could raise a son who was a draft resister?

Another night, and Sorley rose, and walked noiselessly to the shore. It was a miracle he didn't draw fire, but no one sensed him. He began to shout. "Lights! Lights!"

The medic and I hurried to find him, across the glimmering leaves. Mason was already there, in the water beside him; they glowed in the moonlight. I helped them to shore. "Shut up!" Mason said, when the captain began to protest.

"Lights," Sorley explained. "Don't you see the lights, Jonesy? Over there, across the river, in the bamboo there. That's where they are—all this time."

"It's the moon, sir," I told him.

"We've got to report this. Call in artillery. Lieutenant—"

"It's just moonlight," I said. "You see things

that aren't there. They wouldn't give themselves
away like that—they wouldn't use lights. You *never*
see them, sir. Calm down. Please."

"Don't they . . . go in boats?"

"Nosir."

"Oh." He allowed us to guide him back to his
position, where we laid him down, covered him.
Sleepwalking, I thought, but then it hit me that it
wasn't merely that. It wasn't simply nightmares,
not any kind of madness. It was just fear, all mixed
up with his one-armed uncle and the son who'd
taken a forked path—perhaps, too, with his desire
to count for something, and go home a hero.

That was the end. Lieutenant Mason whispered violently on the radio. He woke up the
colonel.

I went down to the Red Cross Club, and slept
through mid-day beneath an air-conditioning
vent. Then I went into the sun.

A gritty wind had risen, shriveling every live
thing. Walking the mile to HQ seemed impossible;
I sat down in the shade of B Company's barracks,
on an overturned bucket, and didn't feel I could
stand again. I was all used up. Nine days left, and
I didn't know what it meant.

A lieutenant with the markings of finance gave
me a ride. He was neat and clean in a way I'd
forgotten how to be; even his dull, Korean-made
boots shone. I watched those boots trying to
speed-shift the jeep: this had been the war for him.

Mortar rounds to either side, and, like Rock Hudson, he'd get us through.

He stopped on the hillside above my HQ. How did he know where I lived? "Good luck to you, Jonesy," he said.

"Thanks," I said. The mystery of how he could know me without my knowing him put me at distance from myself. I stood in the sun, disoriented. Maybe that was how I became human again, I thought. I stopped being Jonesy.

There was a formation below. In the heat everything swirled, but gradually I understood that this was supposed to be my company. They'd thrown me a party and then left for the field, so this group was nothing but cooks, clerks, medics, and of course the shammers—those with minor wounds or the clap, those who got high and stared all day at the lizard on the ceiling. Bodies, to stand more or less erect, and make a ceremony.

What ceremony? There had been no announcement in the morning. I crouched on the hillside, my back to the glare and the desiccating wind, a spy. There was a pale half moon on the horizon, strafed with red grit.

Here were the colonel, Captain Sorley, and a new captain I didn't recognize—a soul brother in starched fatigues and dazzling boots. As the colonel began to speak, six helicopters churned low overhead, bound for the jungle. Their noses dipped in formation, with the moon between them and the sun glinting off their rotor blades: lovely.

I understood. The colonel finished his speech and saluted the black captain, who saluted Sorley and began spitting out admonishments to his stoned troops.

Walking stiffly, but with his trousers hitched too high, and his back slung forward, Sorley accompanied the colonel up the hill, toward a jeep piled high with gear. He saw me, and I stood, wondering if I should salute. "Sir," I said, and stepped back, thinking, he's drunk. Was he? Did he need to be? He stared as though I were from another world. Then, without a word, he jerked up his head and moved on.

Incubation Period

TOWARD EVENING Lansing's squad climbed onto the deuce-and-a-half that would drop them somewhere on the rubber plantation, where they'd set up an ambush for the imaginary enemy.

It had been the routine for nearly five months. Men in other companies had actually seen combat; and at first the stories they told troubled him to the point he couldn't sleep. Now, a seasoned troop himself, the stories struck him as too colorful, too deliberately shocking—cinematic. Their purpose was to provide an escape from the dreariness of army food, army trucks, army damnfool lieu-tenants.

There would be no assault into enemy fire tonight. Instead, Lansing faced another party—a deadly party, to be sure, but at least he could get a little high and sleep for ten hours. It was as though he'd been accepted into the least desirable fraternity on campus. "Why don't you come along, Lieutenant?" some idiot yelled at Greer. "You might get laid."

"Who said that?" Lieutenant Greer, who'd been with them for six weeks, whose own war stories detailed the hardships of his training in Panama, spun dramatically. In the also dramatic silence, Lansing could be a little sympathetic. Open secrets, by definition, were not to be discussed; and if they were, Greer was forced to act surprised.

"If I hear of one man jack in my command consorting with the friendlies—I *mean, getting laid*—you goddam better believe he'll be in the colonel's office at 0800, and we'll slap an Article 15 on him."

Lansing suppressed a laugh. In these woods, an Article 15 had as much force as a string of fire-crackers. As Greer waited, his cheeks seemed to glide up and down in outrage. Then the requisite, chastened "Yessir" returned from the truck, Greer waved at the driver, and they lumbered away.

The ladies had been taking their tea under the eucalyptus trees. As the truck neared, they gathered their gear and leaped onto their Hondas, while the men, looking down at them, variously whooped or assumed the masks of jaded consumers.

A dozen hogs scurried left and right, and the truck slowed to ford a shallow, scummy creek. They climbed, gained speed, and bumped and thundered through the rubber trees, with the sun seeming to roll over and over at the ends of rows, far away.

They made camp in minutes. Lansing lay under the hooch, smoking a joint, with the BBC out of Kuala Lumpur in his ears. Suddenly, Kiwi from Bakersfield bent low. "You want the girl?"

He didn't. Once, in the distant past, he didn't out of principle; and now he didn't because the girls were more boring than checkers. "Girl! Old My, and the pregnant one—"

"New girl. Already paid for. You want?"

"What's wrong with her?"

"Beautiful girl. Love at first sight. But . . . she's Cambodian or something, passing through. The others don't like her. I don't know, man. Who understands these people?"

Lansing saw her now, forty feet away in a last patch of sunlight. Darker than the other women, taller . . . somehow she was reminiscent, in the failing light, of a girl he'd known in college. "No, thanks."

"Please."

"Please? She's got the clap, Kiwi. You pay for her, figure it out, and try to pawn her off on me. Some kind of buddy you are."

Kiwi seemed hurt. "No, man. I really want her, but I got to see my old lady in Honolulu next week. If you . . . I really want her, but if you—"

"You don't want to show up dripping."

"Asshole! Try to do a man a favor. It's just I got to thinking about my old lady, and—"

"You feel guilty? Over here? Guilty?"

"Well, yeah, over here. Guilty. Christ."

"You're sure, absolutely sure, she doesn't have

the clap."

Kiwi snorted and took a step toward the other hooch. "Forget it. I'll talk to Lifer."

But now Lansing crawled out. "No way. Think I'd pass up some luck? I'll do it, I'll do it."

"Don't fucking knock yourself out, man."

He led her to the appointed place: some poncho liners thrown down on the clay. She didn't reply when he spoke, didn't help, didn't hinder, when he held up her arms to remove her blouse. Her dark body kept merging with the night so that momentarily he seemed to be standing by himself—only to be joined by an indifferent, almost alien presence. He regretted his bargain with Kiwi. He wished he'd simply turned over and slept.

He slid her pants down, and, as if the pants had been holding her up, she crumpled, then slowly stretched on her back, like something stunned. When still she didn't speak, or acknowledge him in any way, he wondered if she weren't desperate to allow this. Yes, of course she was. She was passing through, and he was her only means to pay for a ticket. He was weak to continue. He had an impulse to masturbate, throw back his head, howl at the stars.

But then he parted her legs and hovered above her, palms flat beside her shoulders. He sought her eyes. Nothing there but two tiny pricks of starlight, stars themselves. A line of shadow hid her mouth. He dipped into blackness to kiss her.

She wrenched away, murmuring, and he recalled someone in the dormitory saying you weren't supposed to kiss prostitutes. He couldn't recall why, unless it was a travesty of tenderness, as if fucking were meaningless, kissing the real intimacy.

"It's all right," he whispered, giving up. He'd pay the woman again; she needed the money more than he did. He hadn't wanted her anyhow. And now he'd summoned the image of his college girl, saw *her* mouth drawn in the darkness, met *her* reproachful eyes.

With a shriek of indrawn breath, the woman reached up to kiss him—or *something* came out of shadow to claim his mouth—while fingers reached round to trip along his backbone, the pad of each pressing down, dancing on. Surprised, he shoved back against the mouth—with insistence, and a query; but her mouth slipped away.

He grasped her shoulders and rolled until she was atop him. She seemed to have no breasts. She ground against him, but he escaped, and mounted her from behind. She arched like a bow, and he slid his hands up her belly, stopping where her breasts should have been. She rolled, he hung on and plunged—then withdrew while he could. He moaned. He turned, ran a hand down her leg, but she slipped from his reach and into the rustling leaves. He lay looking up at the stars, shivering. With the dew, a phosphorescence had risen in the leaves. She glowed like a ghost from the swamp.

"Jesus, who are you?" he said, as he crawled atop her.

She drew up her legs and locked her ankles below the small of his back, pulling him forward as he thrust, yanking him. Soon he was empty, but she held on. And now she spoke, a long, hoarse, whispered speech, earnest, unintelligible. He murmured in reply. The marijuana whirled in his stomach, and he thought he'd vomit. Inside her still, he felt a stinging. He had a vision of a cavern with bleeding pink walls; every intricate formation disintegrated, oozed down around him in violent reds, sulfurous yellows. He grew hotter and hotter.

At last she released him, her heels slipping slowly down his thighs. The phosphorescence dotted her with a vague, woodsy green. He attempted a ritual kiss, but again she twisted away. "Who *are* you?" he said, feeling vulnerable without his pants. She reached across and plucked at his hair.

With the onset of the dry season, Lansing's company moved into an area where the war was reportedly quite real. Lieutenant Greer displayed a new purpose and grimness. Lansing himself was fearful, wary, sensing a terrible payoff for their long period of grace.

Again, nothing happened. The war seemed like a particularly difficult and boring summer camp, a gathering of Scouts not notably thrifty or brave. If this new country was menacing, it was because of its loneliness, its aura of abandonment.

Once, a wild burst of fire broke out ahead of the column, and Lansing hit the ground, thinking, now, my God, it's happening. But the enemy was a water buffalo, far from water, wandering, too; the point man had fired because of the movement in the brush. The thing stubbornly refused to die, so he and the others emptied several magazines point-blank into its skull. Finally, it sank to its knees, and toppled. Once more there was only the dry air, with birds taking flight far ahead, and then silence.

Several nights before Christmas they waited out a saturation bombing. The ground shook, and the sky fused in white arcs. The company loitered for a day after, waiting for the ground to cool, then made a path between craters, under the twisted, still-smoldering trees. Strewn about were the warm excrescences of deep earth: rock and clay, with molten striations of red and purple, like sores on a vast skin. There was an acrid scent in the dry air, mixed with the smell of burnt flesh. No dead men: just deer, and strange little rodents.

In the night, Lansing had a feverish dream of his father and himself, driving to the induction center. A dark-haired woman turned on the sidewalk, and smiled. Lansing had an erection but tried to show nothing in his face. Soon, he'd face the gravity of war. His father sat beside him.

But his father grinned and winked, and somehow then they were in a room with the woman. Lansing's mother was in the kitchen, singing, while his father stroked the woman thigh. "Come here, son," he said. "Let me show you something."

Lansing woke, scooted toward the foxhole, discovered that he had ejaculated. It was alarming, and shameful, to be so out of control. As he tried to clean himself, he burned with horror not at a dream, but a memory: the Cambodian woman, under the rubber trees. Yes, there would have been an incubation period. While he was camping, his largest problem mere boredom, a secret army, a band of wild saboteurs, rampaged through his flesh.

In the morning he felt no pain, only a weakening, nearly pleasurable sense of being siphoned off. How could this happen to someone as smart as he? He did not understand the disease. Would it make an inexorable progress, or march mysteriously away?

On Christmas Day he stood at Lieutenant Greer's position, controlling an urge to scream. Greer didn't look at him. Sick as he was, Lansing knew that the lieutenant would make him beg.

A helicopter landed in the clearing by the crater, bringing a chaplain and the first portion of the hot Christmas dinner guaranteed every soldier, wherever in the world he served, whether Jew, Christian, or Rosicrucian. Greer turned his dark eyes on Lansing as the helicopter rose, and the rotors of another beat distantly. Lansing reached back for some last vestige of dignity. "I need to go in today, sir."

"You're talking to me?"

"Yes, sir. I've got the clap. I have to go in."

Greer stared toward the crater where the rosy-cheeked chaplain, brandishing a cigar and toting a mailbag, stood in for Santa Claus. Greer shook his head abstractedly, as if Lansing's report concerned the weather. "That's impossible. I *mean* . . . you must have something else. No contact with the friendlies allowed. Have you seen the medic?"

Lansing could barely speak. "He doesn't carry penicillin."

"Could be you have malaria. Have you been taking your pills? The orange one? The little white one?"

"Don't *do* this."

"Let's say you have . . . such a disease. Why didn't you have it treated back on the firebase?"

"There's an incubation period. I didn't know."

"You didn't know you had the clap? I don't believe that, Lansing. I think you're afraid we'll hit some bad shit out here, and you're trying to escape. Let's wait another five days to be sure." He smiled. "So that whatever's incubated . . . *hatches.*"

Lansing bent suddenly at the waist. "I *can't* wait. Shoot me. Keep me that long, you might as well shoot me."

Greer nodded sympathetically. "Maybe you'd care to tell me exactly how it happened. I *mean,* you've put me in an awkward position. The captain will be furious. And there's the goddam paper work, Lansing. Think of that."

Lansing clenched his fists, and threw up his arms. It might have seemed as though he were about to strike Greer, and Greer flinched, but Lansing was reaching into the air for something to grab, something to disperse the pain. *"Man.* I fucked this girl, that's all. The wrong one."

Greer nodded. "Are you ashamed?"

"I'm awful damn sorry."

"There's a reason we don't allow contact with the friendlies, Lansing. These women could over-hear what might seem to you the most innocent remark—"

"She was Cambodian. She didn't understand English."

"Really. How do you know that, soldier? How do you know she wasn't a VC sympathizer? See what I mean?"

Lansing hung his head. He remembered a stray dog he'd adopted when he was a kid. It was a stupid dog that ate a peck of green peaches, then lay under the porch steps, shitting itself to death.

"I don't know anything, sir." Again he grabbed at the air. "Except I'm so sick and I have to go in, *please.*"

And now Greer seem indifferent. "Right. No problem."

Lansing sat heavily on a log. Another heli-copter landed, depositing the rest of the meal and four immaculate Navy men, who each shook the chaplain's hand and then climbed the berm of the crater. Singers, he thought dizzily. They came from somewhere. Their existence made sense.

Greer guided him toward the mess line with

an aura of mock respect, as if what he had here was an honored guest. "Every-body knew what was wrong with you, of course. You've been limping around like a damn cripple. Even if you hadn't asked, I'd have sent you in."

Lansing nodded, his eyes half-closed, the pain transporting him into a new existence. He had to urinate, and didn't know if he could. The navy men sang, with rousing cheer, "White Christmas" and "O Little Town of Bethlehem," as Greer held out the hot meal guaranteed even to a soldier with the clap. "What are you thinking now, Lansing?"

"I'm thinking this can't be war, it's . . . *look* at that. Who *are* they?" He pointed at the navy men.

"Wonderful men. I *mean,* you're surrounded by damn good men. So what happened to you?"

Lansing closed his eyes. "I fucked up, sir."

"You're a disgrace."

Lansing stared. He could, dispassionately, wish this man dead. The world would be a better place, one tiny piece of evil would have been vanquished, if Greer were dead. Lying sprawled on the crater there, shot through the heart, dead. "If you say so, sir."

"I do say so." Greer tore off a piece of turkey and chewed thoughtfully. "You'll never be able to have children, Lansing. I hope you realize that."

He crawled onto the highest bunk, where the light was poor, and tried to sleep. The planes roared outside and dust seeped through the ceil-

and hung forever in the dry, stale air.

Every hour or so he had to urinate. He limped out to the piss tube, and clutched at the pipe above as planes took off, and landed. Once the battalion commander joined him, a big man, a moose. Lansing glanced up, expecting an awful, searing glare, but instead the man laughed.

There were other ghosts in the hooch, who, in the dust-filled light, seemed trapped in an old movie. There was a soft-spoken Georgia boy, a pothead who spent all day strumming his guitar. There was a Puerto Rican with a dirty bandage around his chest, who lay motionless on a bunk piled high with girlie magazines. There was a short, nervous black who seemed always just about to break into violence—and sometimes he did, hitting the walls with his fists, and kicking an empty footlocker.

There was nothing to do but eat, get high, and read porn. No one spoke to him. No news came his way, except one day the nearly violent black said, "You lucky. They in the shit out there. You lucky."

Lucky? The army inside him had retreated. The pain was gone. Would you call that luck? Shyly, Lansing asked the medic if he could have children.

"Man as ugly as you? No fuckin' way."

"Really."

"Well, hell yes. That was *nothin'*. You were lucky—I mean, there was this guy in Delta, he had it shot off. Wa-wa-*wow*, man."

Nothing? Perhaps the pain, which had been something, was even worth it if now he could be as he was, yet wiser. In the meantime, he'd missed the long marches, the bad food. There were just so many days to endure. If he passed some of them here, safely—yes, that was a sort of luck.

He could not escape his nightmares. He dreamed of walking through a company of sleeping men, and calling out to a friend—only to realize the friend was dead.

He dreamed of his girl at college. She drew him aside, and undressed him as her parents looked on. "We can have children," Lansing explained.

He awoke to blinding lights, moans, curses, as the First Sergeant, the XO, and some man Lansing had never met rousted out one of his bunkmates for some obscure midnight duty.

The man Lansing had never met kicked the Georgia boy's feet and said, "Let's go, Fuckhead." In the harsh light, the stranger resembled an upright rat with his long nose, his gleaming black eyes. Lansing turned his head, shutting his eyes to the glare, the curses, the dust newly stirred and floating and settling. "No, no, no, *Je*sus," the Georgia boy said. "Make Johnson go. Not me, man."

"Scumbag," the rat-faced man said. "We got work."

What work? The rat-faced man and First Sergeant staggered off, pulling along the Georgia boy or the Puerto Rican or the nearly violent black. A little later, as if nothing had happened, the lights went out.

First Sergeant asked Lansing to do some typing and said, pleasantly enough, "So you had the clap."

"Well, I—"

"I had it in Korea. I'd a killed the bitch. You wait, you wait, and it comes up and bites you. Teaches you where to dip your wick, huh?"

"Will there be . . . an Article 15?"

"Who told you that?"

"Lieutenant Greer."

"He's just talkin'. Naw. We'd be typin' up half the fuckin' army."

Lansing relaxed. That evening, he had a large meal and sat watching a movie with the medic. He smoked a joint and contemplated the city of hospitals, brightly-lit tonight under the great moon, with the dark mountain behind. He staggered back to the hooch and dropped, at last, into sleep without dreams. He considered that if his luck held, he might become the new company clerk, and serenely wait out the war.

Deep in the night the same pleasant first sergeant and the rat-faced man came in with the dust and rumbling of aircraft. They kicked his feet. He rolled over, and they shone a light in his eyes. "Mom!" Lansing said. "Mom!"

"I look like your mama?" First Sergeant said.

"On your feet, motherfucker," said the rat-faced man.

"What?"

"Get up! You got work to do."

"What work?"

He stumbled out into the night, afraid of being prodded, and struck. Would they shoot him? No, no, they had gone, abandoning him to the darkness. He stood somewhere on the strip, panting. But . . . there were others around him. No one spoke, but a man lit a cigarette, and passed it to him. It was the nearly violent black. "We all right," he said, his voice disembodied. "We all right here."

Banking out of the valley below, dropping down the horizon across the tropical moon, a helicopter bore down as the dust rose. Lansing coughed, and drew a towel to his face. Floodlights shone from every angle, pinpointing an area before them; the helicopter throttled low. "Move! Move it!" called the rat-faced man, a shadow in the dust. And at last Lansing understood: a load of wounded, bleeding, moaning, dead.

With the others, he drew these bodies onto the stretchers, grasped flesh in the dark and raced for the trucks that bore them up the hill toward the bright city. Six helicopters, then seven: a terrible night out there. He journeyed now into the immaculate city, and carried these men, dead and dying, into the light. Inside, on the clean plastic floor, nurses hovering with their tubes and bottles and shining instruments, he thought this might be another of his dreams. For it couldn't be *he*, with his hair matted down, in need of a shave; he'd lost an ear. Couldn't send him home like that, dead. It was Lieutenant Greer, and amid the wildest panic of his young life what Lansing thought was, sweet Jesus, I'm lucky. I'm lucky. I'm lucky.

A Man's World

NO ONE GREETED them. Dotty, her plump boss, beckoned urgently, and Arlene hurried to crouch behind a row of fuel barrels, barely ahead of a storm of grit that strafed the barrels like a minigun. When the helicopter cleared she stood warily, staring at the jungle two hundred yards away. "Just smile," Dotty said, resting a hand on her shoulder. "You'll knock 'em dead."

They grabbed their gear and followed a jagged path through the concertina wire and onto the firebase, passing culverts where the artillery crews slept. Each soldier had a bunk, a footlocker, a PX stereo, and each had taped photographs of his girlfriend or of a centerfold to his rounded steel ceiling. As they passed, Merle Haggard belted out a song, then Aretha Franklin, then Creedence Clearwater Revival.

Left a good job in the city, Arlene murmured, when, suddenly, a howitzer boomed. She dropped to the ground, certain she'd been wounded, and then five howitzers were firing, the grimy, shirtless boys behind them nonchalantly opening chambers when the barrels heaved back, expertly shoving in new shells, dancing forward and back as if they were part of the machinery. A dozen rounds went out while Arlene hugged the dirt, covering her ears. The boys stared but seemed not to see her. The firing ceased and Merle Haggard returned: *Mama tried.*

Dotty motioned irritably. Ashamed of herself, mimicking the same mask of indifference the soldiers wore, Arlene followed her down a sandbagged tunnel that led into the command bunker. In the center of the room a string of naked light bulbs dangled. To their left a man was typing, while another shuffled through a pile of maps. Four enlisted men spoke into radios built into the wall, and a captain moved from one to the other. He nodded curtly. "Afternoon, Dotty. You bring us a movie?"

"Pork Chop Hill."

"You're shitting me." Grinning affably, the captain looked Arlene up and down as he spoke into the microphone. He smacked his lips and Arlene shrank to the wall, feeling like a side of beef in her thin, cotton blouse and pleated skirt. She'd made the mistake, when Dotty asked her what she could do, of saying she used to be a cheerleader.

"Roger, Bandit, gotcha lima chuck," the captain said. "Redleg on its way. ETA three-zero, that's seconds, Bandit, not minutes, how copy?"

Outside, the howitzers began booming again.

"That's all I had this week," Dotty said. *"2001* came in from the marines all chewed up. You ready for us, Don?"

"Squared away." The captain looked unhappy. "Roger, Bandit. Copy: *right* five-zero, *drop* one-zero-zero. Hang in there, pal, Big Daddy's on his way."

A tall man came down the tunnel. He smiled shyly at Arlene out of the shadows, and for an instant she thought of her faraway father. "Good afternoon, ladies," the tall man said.

"Lieutenant," Dotty said neutrally.

The lieutenant picked up Dotty's bird cage and one duffel bag and they filed outside again. The guns were going crazy and Arlene couldn't hear, but the lieutenant nodded toward a sort of amphitheater cleared out between the infantry bunkers, sandbagged all around.

The captain burst out of the CQ. "Dotty, get me Clint Eastwood!" he yelled.

"I put him on order!" Dotty yelled back. "I'm not Superwoman!"

Arlene didn't fault the soldiers for being so filthy. There was no escape from the heat here and that red dust never stopped blowing. When it rained, no doubt the dust turned into a quagmire. Even so, the tall lieutenant's trousers were neatly bloused, his jungle boots polished. His silver bars flashed in the sun. A *first* lieutenant.

She thought of the story she'd read flying in from the States, *Luzon Nurse*. It was about a brave, handsome lieutenant whose wounds were cared for by a confident young nurse, Samantha Peterson.

Of course, the Red Cross strictly forbade involvements. It happened, sometimes, but you'd be on your way to Oakland before the day was out if you were discovered. The rule was for your own protection. When the ratio of men to women was one hundred to one, you couldn't be too careful.

"I'll bet you're from Iowa," the lieutenant said.

If she looked straight ahead, she could imagine her father walked beside her, since this man was just as tall and spoke in the same quick way. But there was no green pasture before them, no gleaming little pond with geese on it. "Nebraska," she said wistfully. "How can you tell?"

"You look so . . . innocent."

"Well, I'm *new*." She was a little offended. "You make innocence sound sinful."

He laughed and extended a hand. "My name's Henry Stiles. I'm from Mitchell, South Dakota."

She wanted to know everything about him. She wanted to tell him how homesick she was, how helpless she sometimes felt. "Arlene Kessler. I'm from the Sand Hills. We're practically neighbors."

"*Stay* innocent," he whispered. He had serious blue eyes, Arlene thought, full of sadness. She wanted to comfort him, to tell him he'd make it through this terrible time, just as, when her mother died, she'd brought her father through the miserable winter. She was here on earth to offer comfort, and, when she'd finished with Vietnam, she planned to get her degree in social work, and work on the Rosebud Reservation.

Dotty set up her felt-covered stand, and donned her cape and top hat, while the lieutenant went off to round up an audience. Arlene stood not knowing what to do, sweat running down her dusty legs. When the firing ceased a dozen men straggled in, and sat cross-legged or hoisted themselves up on piles of sandbags.

The last man stumbled into the circle as if he had been pushed. His skin was streaked with dirt and there was a tear in his trousers. Lieutenant Stiles, his lips tightly clinched, followed shortly behind him. "Sit down, Hays," he told the straggler. "Enjoy yourself."

Dotty made her pitch for the Red Cross Club. "Come as you are," she said, which drew a laugh. "All the Kool-Aid you can drink, and it's air-conditioned!"

She pulled a quarter from behind her ear, then palmed it into a multi-colored Japanese fan. She juggled four cans of Black Label, ending by throwing the beer to her audience.

The boy named Hays played in the dirt with his pocketknife, never once lifting his eyes. When he twisted the knife his biceps and chest muscles flinched beneath his soiled tee shirt, but he didn't seem strong. He was pale—wrenched—as if he'd had a bout with hepatitis.

For her finale Dotty drew a dove from a black cloth. The dove fluttered up and perched on her shoulder, and there was a chorus of "Peace!" Arlene did three flips across the tarpaulin, arching her hips each time: she was Betty Grable, Ann-Margret. On her third landing she slipped and skidded into Hays. Her legs spread around his lean belly and she banged into his nose. "Sorry," she whispered.

"Don't *waste* it, lady," said a man with a blistered face and a bushy red mustache.

"At ease, soldier!" Henry said harshly, and drew Arlene to her feet. She stumbled against him.

"Oh, lieutenant," the same man said. "You're *so* strong."

But the soldiers were applauding now, and Arlene threw out her hands, and bowed. Hays looked up, too, but not with gratitude, or amusement. What was in those eyes? Not anger, exactly.

"Something wrong with him?" Arlene asked, as Hays shuffled off.

Henry's eyes narrowed. "He just got out of the stockade."

"For?"

Henry shrugged, implying it was none of her business.

Dotty nodded a goodbye or two and strode purposefully toward the helicopter pad, leaving

Arlene the heavier of the duffel bags. Lord help me, she thought, realizing that her dumb cartwheels had upstaged her boss. She'd be stuck at the club for six months, baking cookies and smiling, smiling, smiling when her heart was breaking. She carried the duffel bag for a hundred feet in the heavy air, until her neck and cheeks dripped sweat. She dropped the bag, and dragged it.

She saw the lieutenant from afar, pointing angrily at one of the crews in a firing pit, striding quickly over to do the job himself. She paused on the berm, waiting for him to turn, smiling at him pointedly. Sometimes, you just had a feeling, rules or no rules. When Dotty threw her a meaningful look and pointed at the incoming helicopter, Arlene bent to tie her shoe.

Just in time, Henry saw her and trotted over. "We rotate back to Tay Ninh in ten days," he shouted.

"I can't actually—"

But then he was gone and she sat in the helicopter again. Dotty stared at her without expression and then fastened her eyes on the green horizon, where rounds streaked out and exploded in the tall trees. "I thought that went well," Arlene called out, but the rotors had powered up, and her words were lost in the wind.

Dotty had flown to Pleiku to open a new club, leaving Arlene in charge of her fool's agenda, which, in six weeks, was how Arlene had come to think of it.

By 0800 Beulah and she had baked three hundred oatmeal, chocolate chip, and peanut butter cookies, and made two pots of coffee and a twenty-gallon canister of lime Kool-Aid. They placed their offerings neatly on white tablecloths with stacks of red paper plates and napkins with green helicopters on them, and by then there were thirty men at the door.

First, they swooped down on the cookies. Then the television went on to Armed Forces reruns: *Bonanza,* followed by *Combat!* and *Have Gun Will Travel.* Meantime, the sounds of a pool game—the clinking balls, the stream of profanity, the occasional cheer—rose up in a competition, the black soldiers trying to dominate, the whites arriving, en masse, to give challenge. A fight was always about to break out.

White or black, in Arlene's estimation, they were the scum of the earth. Short of calling in the MPs, she couldn't control them, and calling the MPs meant paperwork and a lecture from Dotty. "The greatest service is given in the face of hostility," was one of her lines, but the greatest hostility was served up to Arlene.

"Put your little twat right here, sugar!"

A week before, when three of them chanted "Bimbo! Bimbo! Where you gonna go-ee-o?" she ran back to the kitchen, and gave in to tears. When she'd joined the Red Cross she'd visualized holding the hands of dying soldiers, writing letters to their saintly mothers, but the truth was that she might as well have been ministering to prisoners.

"You don't really know what they're going through," Dotty told her. "You don't know the effect you're having. You're a pretty girl, Arlene. There may be times when just looking at you pulls these soldiers back from despair."

In some other war, Arlene thought. On some other planet.

Her only friend was Beulah, a plain woman with whom no one flirted, a Jehovah's Witness whose facial expression had frozen somewhere between disapproval and pain by the age of nineteen. You got the feeling, if her eyes crossed yours, that the end was near.

Not that Beulah was truly frightening. In fact, she faded away into some deeply personal misery whenever Arlene attempted conversation. But, in her shapeless blue smock, Beulah invoked the drab memories of these men, of foster mothers and welfare workers and psychiatric nurses. The very people they would go all the way to Vietnam to avoid. "Game time!" Beulah yelled out, as if games were the daily sedative. She clapped her hands, and the echo was like AK fire. "Game time!"

Then Arlene—cast, for lack of a better candidate, as girl-next-door—smiled brightly and said, "This will be so much *fun!*"

Which was the knock-out punch that sent the worst of her troublemakers scurrying out the back door, less from intimidation than disgust. Those who remained were merely cannon fodder, the dunderheads, the potheads, the sleepyheads, men who judged any day they avoided being shot at as a good day.

"Do we have any volunteers?" Arlene said, pacing in the center of the day room, glaring with mock-menace at one and then another, stopping, at last, before a sleeper who'd covered his face with an old *Newsweek*.

"Shhh!" she said, as laughter rippled among her troops. She slid toward the sleeper with long, exaggerated strides, like a cartoon villain. Only a giggle or two interrupted the quietness.

She motioned to two soldiers to come in from behind. Then she pounced, knocking aside the *Newsweek*, bringing her finger down on the soldier's nose. "Sleeper!" she hissed, and laughter erupted.

The sleeper jerked up his head in panic, and brought his hands to his face as if to ward off an attack. Now the laughter was like a wall that encircled Arlene and her victim, but she knew she'd made a mistake. The sleeper was the baffled young man from the firebase, Hays.

His eyes held the same wild glint, but he recognized her, and seemed to relax a little. "It's okay," she whispered, leaning near, at the same time motioning to her volunteers. They lifted Hays in his chair and carried him to the center of the room. He shrank back and the color in his face fled. His legs went slack.

Laughter rose again, as Beulah handed Arlene her scepter and fastened the red cape around her shoulders. "I am Princess Arlene!" she announced, and her subjects stomped the floor and beat on wastebaskets.

Oh, but those eyes! They were not just wild, but red, and sunken in his pale face. Stop, she told herself, and glanced up at Beulah, but Beulah stood with folded arms, her face inscrutable, a sphinx. And a regiment of faces cheered her on. "What's your name, soldier?"

"Elwood Hays," he said, with a flat drawl. Oklahoma, she thought, or Texas.

"Elwood, you're a handsome man!"

"Whoa, babe!" a big sergeant said. "She loves you!"

Arlene touched Hays' shoulder with the scepter. "But, Elwood, you've been *bad!*"

"He been wicked!"

Elwood looked miserable. Didn't he know that his reward was a kiss? She'd have begged him if she could, held his hand, listened all night if he was able to talk. And, for an instant, she thought that they silently communicated, one chastened soul to another.

"You were sleeping, Elwood! You men, wasn't he sleeping?"

"Yeah! Yeah!"

"And what do we do with a sleeping soldier?"

"Take him out and shoot him."

"Naw," said one of the pool sharks. "Fuck the man *blind.*"

Arlene swallowed. "No, no, please," she managed. "Let's be nice here. We make our sleepers play *games.*"

She motioned to Beulah, who stepped behind Hays and deftly blindfolded him. He tensed as if he would bolt, but Arlene dropped a hand to his shoulder. "It's okay, Elwood, it's nothing," she whispered, and then, to her cheering audience, called out, "This is a taste game, Elwood. Maybe you played it back in school."

His blindfolded head rolled like a chicken's, seeking her voice. "Mrs. Dedman's class."

He was cooperating, Arlene thought. This would work out, and the worst of her day would be done, and she could go to lunch. "Good! Now, you play the game really well, Elwood, you get a prize. Okay?"

"Okay," he said, his arms pulled back to his chest again, as if to protect himself from—from what? His stance was that of a man about to be beaten. Arlene glanced at Beulah, who shrugged and handed her the dill pickle.

"Oh, no," came a chorus.

"That's a big one!" said a short man, who leaped up to a water pipe and chinned himself three times.

Arlene thrust the pickle into Hays' mouth, plunged it forward and back once, all to a cascade of laughter. Hays swallowed and involuntarily bit down.

"Well?" Arlene said.

Hays twisted his head and spat out the pickle. He rose in the chair but Beulah pressed him back.

"What's wrong with you, young private?" said

the man doing chin-ups. He jumped down and walked several yards on his hands.

"You sposed to guess," said the pool shark. "What it *is*."

"One more, Elwood, okay?" Arlene whispered. Some of the men were slipping away, but she didn't care, it was almost over. She grinned and walked about the chair bent like Groucho Marx, her royal cape swirling. Then she pushed the spoonful of chocolate pudding into Hays' mouth.

But this time he leapt up, sweeping his arms wildly, knocking the spoon and bowl from Arlene's hands. He yanked off the blindfold and crouched, his eyes jerking about. He panted like a dog.

"Elwood, please!" Arlene said.

When she reached to calm him he swept his arm back, catching her on the neck. She skidded in the pudding and fell to the floor, and, in that instant, realized she'd seen those eyes once before, long ago, when her father shot a pig for butchering. The thing knew it was dying, but kept staggering. You could see betrayal in those eyes, and the doom of the world.

"Jesus," said the little man who did chin-ups, and he and the pool shark tried to restrain Hays. But Hays threw out his arms furiously, dropping blows right and left. The men parted as if a tiger were among them, and, in seconds, Hays was gone.

Beulah held out a hand, and Arlene rose slowly to her feet. She ran to the door and stared down the red road. The heat howled before her, filled with red dust, impenetrable. "Elwood Hays," she murmured. "I'm so sorry."

She lived in a tiny trailer uphill from the club, tucked into a bend in the road so that everything not bolted down vibrated when trucks went by on their way to the motor pool. But she had a shower, a hotplate, even a small refrigerator. Every night she wrote her father, had a bowl of soup and an apple. Sometimes, she tried to read. Then she closed all the windows, drew every curtain, and turned the air conditioner to high. Without the three alarms she placed by her bed she would not have known when day had come, when to go to work.

More than once, cocooned in her blankets, exhaust from the air conditioner flooding over her toes, she visualized Lieutenant Henry Stiles standing in the little hall. She drew back her legs as he yanked on the sheets. "Where have you been?" she asked. "Why didn't you call?"

And, sometimes, she heard her father coming up the back steps, stumbling about by the narrow hall closet, dropping his chore boots. Soon he'd be upstairs, shaving for his job at the hardware, looping his one tie over his head and knotting it, muttering about his pigs. A diminished and befuddled man, now that his wife was gone. "Arlene, get up!" he'd call. If she failed to rise, he'd come in and pinch her big toe, and she'd laugh and laugh and laugh, as if she were still six and there were happy times in the old house.

Bang!

She fell to the floor, dragging her bedclothes with her. She lay in the blackness and heard something click on the tile: a roach. She came to her feet, bobbed dizzily, felt for her thongs and housecoat.

Bang!

Someone was at the door. At 0230? Rocking the trailer with blows? She edged down the hall, afraid to turn on a light. She glided to the little jalousie window, cranked it, and made out a bulky shape on her steps. She couldn't tell who it was, or even *what* it was.

Bang! Bang! Bang!

She picked up the knife lying on the counter and slipped into the living room. She stood just inside the door, trying not to breathe, and now she heard the man make animal sounds, in a muttering that resolved once or twice into almost-words.

"Hee-upp," she thought he said. And then "ma'am," she recognized "ma'am." It was a southern voice: Elwood Hays.

She tried to speak but her mouth refused to shape words. Or maybe she screamed, because, later, she could never perfectly recall. Lights crisscrossed the trailer and she dropped again to the floor. An engine roared, and there were shouts. Gears clashed. Then there were voices again, and a burst of automatic fire that hammered into the trailer, shaking it top to bottom. Hays grunted like a pig. This time, the firing sounded as though it were inside the trailer—inside her head, tearing her brains apart.

More firing, still, but sporadic. Hays screamed into her ear, and, from afar, soldiers cursed him by name, and cursed fate.

"Ah, shit," she heard.

The lights went out and there was a long silence. She lay paralyzed on the floor, shivering with cold, instructing herself to rise, but unable to. She thought of the root cellar, long in disuse, hidden by sapling cottonwoods, where she used to play when she was a little girl. Her secret place.

At last the gears clashed again and the jeep whined away. She heard a voice she knew. "Arlene, are you there?"

"Yes," she said, with all her strength, but only a whisper came out. Her alarm clock buzzed. She drew herself to her knees, and stood unsteadily on her bare feet. Where had she put her thongs?

"Lieutenant Stiles?" she said. "Henry?"

"Let me in!"

She unbolted the door and fell against him. He was sweating, and smelled of tobacco. He lay her on the couch, and the little room spun around one bright light. He handed her the tea he made on her hotplate.

"He's dead? He's dead?"

Henry nodded grimly. "When he fired into the trailer, there wasn't much we could do. We had to stop him somehow."

"Why?"

"He was on guard, high on something, I said I

was gonna take him in. And he snapped. He started running. Down the road, we lost him for a while. Then we caught him in the spotlight."

"Why here?"

Henry hesitated. "You'd have to ask Hays. I— *we* thought he meant to kill you."

"He seemed so gentle," she murmured.

She closed her eyes, and, when she opened them, it seemed as if hours had passed. Henry looked like her father in the weak light. Of course, her father never talked about playing basketball in Mitchell, South Dakota, how he'd almost had a scholarship.

She wanted to ask him why he hadn't called, to tell him about the letters she'd written him here in her cold cell, but never sent. Hays wasn't really dead, was he? Was a man dead, and on her doorstep? What had Hays done, she wondered, because in that game, you remember that silly game? It was like something terrible had happened to him, you know what I mean, Henry?

"I know," he whispered, as he carried her down the hall, her legs freezing even though, outside, she knew it was unbearably hot. She dropped to her sheets a thousand miles below, as if she were drugged. "Stay," she told him, forgiving his neglect because he had saved her, believing in him because she believed in America, in noble nurses, in brave lieutenants.

He undressed and slipped beside her, squeezing her breasts against his bare chest. *Oh love oh love oh careless love,* she sang deliriously, never opening her mouth, as waves of cold delight rushed through her. "I'm 10,000 miles from home," she cried out.

"Shhh," her father said. "Sleep now."

At 0600 there was no sign of him. Even her tea cups had been washed and put away. Nothing remained but the faint smell of tobacco. Kools, she remembered. Henry smoked Kools.

Her hair was tangled. She washed it and combed it carefully and drank tea, shivering in the frigid air.

Then she strapped on a mini-skirt like a sidearm, and marched down the steaming board-walk to the club. When the officers at the CQ called out a gentlemanly good morning, she smiled. When the medics at the AID station whistled, she smiled. When the Vietnamese wo-men looked up from their tubs of boiling blue water, and glowered, she smiled. She was a pretty girl, and she'd been sent here to smile. Because, just like Dotty said, you never knew the effect you were having.

Yet, as the days passed and Henry did not return, one thing began to puzzle her. Why were the bullet holes in her trailer slanted sideways, downhill toward those conex containers? If Hays had intended to kill her, surely he'd have shot directly into her door. She tried to remember all the different bursts of fire she'd heard, tried to reason out who had stood where.

She couldn't confide in Dotty about Henry. But she did mention the game she'd played with

Hays, and how, looking back, she should have realized how troubled he was.

"You couldn't have known that," Dotty said. "You're a woman, not a mind-reader."

Arlene was sure, at least, that lieutenants such as the ones in novels did not exist. Nor was she reading minds when, fully a month later, it at last occurred to her what Elwood Hays had been trying to say. She was sitting in the mess hall after the work day, drinking tea and writing a letter to her father. She looked up at the ceiling fan and the whispering blades had something of the sound of Hays' voice in them.

She covered her face with her hands so that no man could see her tears. "Help," the fan whispered. "Help. Help. Help."

Tanks

THE TANKS were pulled into a circle with their howitzers pointed out, as though Indians were expected. Around the circle stood a field of grass tall as a man but uniform as a wheat field, rolling out almost a kilometer to the jungle wall. The jungle hulked over the grass in a long curve to the horizon, and you couldn't see into it. It seemed more black than green, a wet, cold place that Porter was glad to be even this far removed from. Behind the jungle was an orange glow, and surely that would be the sun, the one that had already been to Missouri.

Porter awoke shivering, his bedroll crested with dew, his neck aching. The dawn was clear but of course it would rain, just like yesterday and the day before. He lay watching Okie, who knelt by the inside track of the point team's Sheridan. "Mornin'," he said, holding out a handful of red clay. "Look at this, Porter. Just like Oklahoma."

"Maybe you could buy a farm here." Porter buttoned his shirt and pulled on his boots, then threw his poncho liner atop the tank to dry. He picked up his rifle from where his bed had been, and propped it across his pack, barrel down. "Damn, it's cold."

"Warm up soon enough."

He followed Okie toward the chow line, massaging his neck and wondering if he could pass another day without shaving. Maybe, unless no orders came down and they were stuck here, in which case Lieutenant Wolfe would make them all shave in the interest of morale. Morale wasn't so much low as hung over: every evening, there was a party until two. He himself, with only sixty-four days to go, was on the wagon.

He stretched his arms toward the sky. Dear God it was a beautiful morning, even if he'd been standing on the moon. If a man could wake up somewhere, and not have a thing to do . . . meet Chris for lunch, take in a movie. A smell hit him like a dream. "They got bacon!"

They stood far back in the line. "Maybe," Okie said. "I cain't see nothin' but that fuckin' grapefruit juice."

"That powdered stuff they mix up, like Tang? The astronauts drink that for breakfast."

"There it is. We gonna fly away, oh glory."

The tank commander broke through the line between them, his plate heaped high with bacon and—even more miraculous, because they'd survived yesterday's long ride—two eggs, sunny-side up. Porter reeled slightly, thinking his whiskers were too long, but the commander passed without an "Excuse me" or even a raising of his eyes.

"Jerk," Okie muttered.

Porter shrugged. "At least they feed us good."

In the month since they'd been attached to armored the commander had not been seen to speak to any of the infantry except Captain Diemer, who rode along atop the commander's track like some captured chief. Diemer was a tall, grave man, a West Pointer who took every wound and death personally. The commander was short and nearly bald and—his own men said—had barely made it through OCS. He'd been dragged kicking and screaming from some sleepy little fort down in Texas. Ah, but status! The armored had it—and nothing was lower than infantry.

Attaching them to armored had been Jolly Green's—the colonel's—idea: more firepower, more kills. He flew over every day, a businessman checking on his investment. He seldom landed, instead calling down coordinates of where the enemy was suspected to be; and sometimes, he flew ahead of them, like a general on a horse. Toward noon chow he dropped low, swooped back over them, and banked into the sun.

The infantry, needing camouflage to be whole, rode high for all to see, clutching at gear, hanging on. The rain scratched their eyes and the steel plate bruised their bones until, like so many RVs in a caravan, the tanks parked in another broad field. As long as they avoided contact, Porter was content, but he understood why grunts felt superfluous. Rifles and trip flares, even Claymore mines, were ridiculous things, alongside the offense a tank could muster. An enemy needed to be both crazy and high to charge across an open field, into howitzers and .50 caliber machine guns.

The infantry was used to silence, and all the shouting, the great engines revving, helicopters coming and going, seemed sacrilegious. After dark stereos blasted away—enough to frighten away the Devil himself.

Black men danced, moaned in communion, shook fists at the moon. Good old boys strummed battered PX guitars, and sang about no-good women.

Breakfast finished, a second cup of coffee in hand, Porter began writing a letter to Trudy, a girl from his mother's church. He dated her several times the summer before he was drafted—the same summer his true love, Chris, hitchhiked to Seattle, flowers in her hair. He wanted to write Chris, not Trudy, but at least Trudy was there.

Her letters arrived regularly, in colored, perfumed envelopes that often had been torn open. She spoke of how fascinating his father's business was—the parts business, genuine NAPA parts. He could see their long, dull future together, and yet he crept up on a proposal of marriage. "Dearest Trudy, if I make it through this, I want you to know that—"

He stopped. She'd accept, and he wouldn't die. Trudy only *seemed* like an abstraction. In sixty-four days, she'd be perfectly real. "Fuckit," he said, crumpling his letter—and Trudy's, too.

It was hot now. He opened a can of apricots and chugged the syrup. "Hear about sergeant yet,

Okie?"

There was a vacancy. Lieutenant Wolfe joined them, and the platoon sergeant left, almost six weeks before. Okie was a logical choice, though so was Snowball—at least when he wasn't stoned.

"It ain't come through yet," Okie said. He slid the bolt of his rifle back and forth, and spread a drop of oil with one finger. "I asked Wolfe, only he gave me the runaround."

"You'll get it. You're due, man."

"Yeah."

Porter lay back against his pack. Nothing would happen until Jolly Green flew over, and lots of men were catching naps, before the sun grew too merciless. His eyes fell to Snowball, sitting atop the gun team's tank twenty meters away.

Snowball waved awkwardly. "Hey, babes," he called out. "We're lonely in the gun team. How come you don't come see us no more?"

"Yeah. Don't mean nothin."

"Come on over tonight, babes. We get fucked up good. Short-timers, am I wrong, am I right?"

"You *right*," Porter called out. Maybe he'd join that group again, and float away with Hendrix and James Brown. He wasn't sure. Snowball and he arrived in-country together, and were soon best friends, but they hadn't spoken for days.

Something went awry when they left for the rear, both bound for R. & R.. Porter tried to talk Snowball into going to Australia, but every night he hung out with the shammers, all of them black—jive-ass niggers, Okie called them. Anyhow it was a group Porter couldn't join. He left for white man's country, while Snowball went to Bangkok; Snowball returned with the clap, and Porter with the notion he might marry Trudy.

Now Snowball talked to Dover, a black man, and several of the black armored. It was a private party, though nervous little Billy Boy seemed to belong, blue eyes and all. Billy Boy smoked dope recklessly, even in daytime, and on patrols if you didn't watch him. Now, atop the tank, he pirouetted to music, hands fluttering in a vaguely feminine way. The blacks, shirts off, sitting cross-legged or lying prone to sun themselves, clapped for Billy Boy, who at last stumbled and plopped heavily beside his buddy Dover.

These days Porter kept company with Okie and Preacher. He hadn't learned the names of the new men in the platoon; he didn't want to. Sometimes, he turned his head to see one of them staring, in a mixed awe and challenge. What a shock to think that he'd become the old pro.

"Good morning, Preacher," he said. Preacher tried to smile.

Breakfast finished, he was having devotions. Lately he pursued the perfection of his soul with a frenzy, reading—muttering—his New Testament all day long, kneeling to pray when the sun went down and marijuana smoke filled the air and men sang and danced in a cacophony only a circle or two removed from fiery hell.

Preacher's eyes had taken on an intensity, his

face a pallor, that made sober men avoid him. In March, before they joined the armored, Cherokee platoon blew up three North Vietnamese coming down a trail—spooks in the night, suddenly lit up, as if with a camera's flash, by a trip flare and exploding Claymores. Dried fish rained in the camp, and Preacher went balmy, screaming that soon Jesus would return.

As if to confirm his prophecy, lightning quaked on the horizon, lending a yellow outline to dark clouds. Lieutenant Wolfe screamed at him, and at last struck him, before Preacher understood how dangerous his antics were. Not the antics, perhaps, but the noise. His eyes held a wound ever since. He'd become a sort of outcast.

Helplessly, he witnessed to Porter. Porter nodded absently, having grown up with the gospel—and his mother, and Trudy. He calculated how much time he had remaining in the field: drop ten days for a leave, another ten to process out, only forty-three days. "Yes, yes," he said, responding to some prompt of Preacher's.

Preacher must have concluded that the moment for Porter's redemption was at hand, for now he went on more intensely, even stammering in his eagerness, at last, in a sort of triumph, asking, "Are you an atheist?"

Heavy artillery. It was hard to conceive of anyone so depraved—or certain—who'd answer, "Yes," while an uneasy, "Well, no . . . " brought the opportunity to kneel, and confess every misery. "I'm a Democrat," Porter said.

Okie laughed aloud, while Preacher looked as if he'd been shot, and turned away. Porter was a little sorry, and wished for something else to say to Preacher, whom he liked.

The three of them fell silent. Having postponed it as long as he could, Porter lit a Pall Mall, and then another. Looking out, he thought of a cool place on the Gasconade River, a bluff off which he dropped a line for crappie and white bass. And then he lifted his head to a shout, a clanking, as if waking from a dream.

He saw a crane. It was huge, with a white neck; except for the black tips of its white wings, it was white. With the early sun, the damp-looking jungle, it suggested a cool pastoral; its wings seemed to sweep in time with the rolling grass. It flew low, ponderously. *"Caree . . . caree . . . "* it sang.

It crossed the sun, wild and orange and over-sized, *holding* the crane. There had been such moments in Missouri, on land so backward Porter thought he was the first to come calling . . .

"Jesus," Okie said, softly. The three of them had stood to watch the crane, but now the dream was over: Billy Boy raised his rifle, thumbed it to automatic, and let fly six rounds.

Porter was amazed. Of course! If you had a gun you could shoot it. It hadn't occurred to him. Stunned, he nodded stupidly as Preacher stepped forward, raised a hand like a prophet, and shouted, "Don't shoot that bird!"

But all the perimeter joined in. Men leaped upon the tanks and wheeled the .50 Calibers around. The morning roared alive. The crane flew past the sun, seemed to hang in the air before a dead tree, the only one on the plain.

Then it fell. Officers ran up, to protest the firing, but it had already ceased.

Porter and Okie sat in the shadow of their Sheridan, sipping iced grapefruit juice. Preacher was asleep: mouth open, glasses askew, forehead glistening. All was quiet.

Across the perimeter, Wolfe stood to stretch periodically, as if to put an idea in motion, but then he consulted the sky, and sat again.

Jolly Green's delay was unusual, poising the day between dread and hope. Dread of a bad mission; hope for another twenty-four hours without risk. Maybe they'd get a hot lunch, Porter thought drowsily, and a siesta—even a shower under that blimp hoisted up by the wrecker track.

He sighed. Maybe another letter from Trudy.

"You like Ann-Margret?" Okie asked.

Porter yanked himself back to consciousness. "Sure."

"I been sittin' here thinkin'. They oughtta fix it up, you get back to the World, you can have any movie star you want."

"Wouldn't be any fun. Those movie stars are miserable."

"The hell. All that money? Wild parties?"

"Take it from me, man: Ann-Margret's miserable."

"How the fuck do you know?"

Dover crossed to Wolfe's position, huge grasshoppers leaping before him in the smashed-down grass. His uniform was clean, and his damp brown cheeks were smoothly shaven. He carried all of his gear.

He reached Wolfe and turned his back, propping his pack on the end of his rifle barrel. In a moment Wolfe shook his head angrily.

"He's tryin' to get out early on his R. & R.," Okie said.

"Good luck."

"He ain't so much as said hello to me in three weeks, then he comes over this mornin', while you and Preacher was sleepin', and wants *me* to talk to Wolfe. He says his little gal friend got her signals crossed, and she's already in Honolulu. I said, sorry, brother, you know Wolfe won't go for that. Give you extra days, don't you wish! He ain't that stupid."

"Even I coulda come up with a better story."

"I ain't callin' him a liar. He showed me her letter. But man, you know well as I do the army don't make no accommodations. That gal can fuckin' wait. What pisses me off, it ain't just that he's black as sin, but he's got the nerve, you know? Snowball wouldna tried that."

Porter sighed. "Snow's actin' kinda strange lately."

"Thinks he's a fuckin' leader of men. But listen to me, Porter, speakin' a Dover. You're a level-headed guy, I'm gonna ask you something."

"I'm just a stupid grunt, man."

"You're alive, ain't you? No shame in bein' infantry. I'm askin' you, what you think, 'bout Dover and this little white girl?"

"Aw, man. Don't get off on this."

"I just think there's two races, that's all. You take, where my daddy used to work, they was this colored man, sweet old man. Only along come the N. double-A. C. P., and you cain't even *talk* to him."

At college Porter cut classes with Chris to attend anti-war rallies. The strength of his convictions had much to do with the brand-new marvels of sex, but anyhow, left over in the revolutionary air, was the black cause. To say you'd joined the march to Selma was a distinction very nearly as powerful as having attended a Beatles concert. Thus Okie's talk was like a reproach to his college days—and even of his lost love. "You can't go around sayin' stuff like that, Okie. Stuff like that, I mean, it's all settled. Dover's fine when the shit flies, huh?"

Okie pointed triumphantly. *"Look.* I told you Wolfe wasn't that stupid."

Wolfe rose quickly, and strode away from Dover, shaking his head. Jolly Green or no Jolly Green, he appeared to have reached a decision about something else as well, something more than a directive to shave, Porter guessed. He felt a mild panic, but he'd been well-behaved for weeks, straight enough for a promotion. Wasn't he already a point man, the unluckiest thing you could be?

One of Wolfe's oddities: when he took command he immediately concluded that Porter was the best point man he had, despite Porter's conviction that he'd have made a fine company clerk. He begged for a clerk's or any other rear job, or to carry ammo behind Snowball—even to take the radio. Nothing less than a bullet could change Wolfe's mind.

Wolfe motioned to Porter and Okie, to the gun team and second squad. Porter picked up Preacher's glasses from the grass, and shook the man awake. "Powwow time," Porter said.

Preacher rubbed his eyes. "Should I bring the radio?"

"No, no. Somethin's up, though."

They ambled across the perimeter, grasshoppers leaping around them, heat hanging down on their clothing. To move was to sweat, and they stopped to wait.

"How many days you got?" Okie asked.

"Sixty-three and a wake-up. Short."

"That ain't short."

"I'm shorter than copperhead snake, fucker."

"I'll be back on the block smokin' see-gars 'fore you make it to Bien Hoa."

"You're gonna re-up, Okie. What you got to

go home for, since Jody got your girl? That old broken-down Cream-O?"

"Camaro, troop. And watch your mouth. That car is some very hot poop."

Lieutenant Wolfe shook his head, and motioned them away. Porter looked up.

Here came Jolly Green.

His bird thundered down the long field, low, fast, its rotors echoing off the jungle walls. It pulled back in the air as if reined in, then touched the ground without a jolt, in time with the earth's motion. The pilot, only a silhouette behind the windshield's glare, now flipped back his helmet, and sat smoking.

Lieutenant Wolfe's cheeks jerked involuntarily. Had he wanted to be a warrant officer, to make daring rescues, be weighted down with wounds and medals? Nothing, Porter thought, was lower than infantry.

Jolly Green stepped from the bird exactly as it touched down, barely bending his head beneath the rotor blades. He wasn't Captain Kirk, miraculously materializing. He was more like a game show host: cool, immaculate, quickly conquering the stage. He barely bent his head beneath the rotor blades, and his cap stayed on—while Diemer and the track commander crouched like refugees.

Jolly Green wrung their hands, and threw an arm around each. Such a big man! He walked them around and around the bird, and they followed like children who had been on their own, and done well, but now were reminded of their true worth, before their angry, purposeful father.

Jolly Green produced a map, which Diemer and the commander held up, while Jolly Green struck with his grease pencil. He pointed down the field, and made complicated notions with his hands. Diemer shouted a question, and so did the commander. Jolly Green shook his head impatiently, then nodded approvingly.

"What the fuck," Okie said.

Now Jolly Green shook hands and jerked away toward the command bird; left so suddenly behind, the two officers seemed small, and shabby. Jolly Green held up a thumb, then looked straight ahead, and it was as if he had already left the earth. The bird ripped away at what seemed full speed. Its wind blew the glass flat; paper plates left over from breakfast sailed toward the jungle.

With everyone else, Porter lifted his head toward the sky, toward the gleaming, mechanical bird. It occurred to him that if a crane could be shot from the sky, so could a helicopter. How splendid to see it drop like a spear! He raised his rifle, and lowered it.

"Two things," said the lieutenant. He moved his hands in precise ways, forcefully, like Porter's high school basketball coach. "First, at 0600 hours this morning, a Chinook cargo bird passed over this grid . . . " He slashed at a point on his map with a grease pencil. "About ten kilometers from here. They monitored a strong radio signal."

Wolfe paused to seek eye contact. The movies, Porter thought; they nestled inside everyone. He too yearned to make a grand speech, at a pivotal moment.

He grinned at Snowball, who looked away; and then Porter turned toward Okie. Okie chewed gum and nodded emphatically, as if he already knew what Wolfe was about to say.

"The signal might have come from a relay transmitter to the North—no sweat. Probably wouldn't be anybody there. But Battalion thinks it could be that regimental headquarters you've all heard about, and I think you know what that means. Boocoo Charley. A regular shitload of gooks."

This brought questions, protests, but Wolfe shook his head. He took an apologetic tone. "I don't know any more, men. Nobody does. Except that we're moving out in twenty minutes." He dropped his voice—again like Porter's coach, just before the game. "Get—your shit—together."

Porter thought he detected a note of doubt in the man's eyes. Genuine worry? So many times Battalion hyped things, and only a long hot ride resulted.

Everyone talked—angrily, bitterly, fearfully, but there was also a cautious enthusiasm in the air, a rising energy. Hearing "twenty minutes," some began to move away, only to stop; Wolfe had said "two things." Porter didn't move. Wolfe had his attention.

There had been other moments such as this, when after heroic deliberation the man arrived at a decision that was almost intellectual. Here it was, then, Wolfe's little masterpiece of bad timing. Like the dead crane, it added to the wrongness of the day. Wolfe took a cheery, camp counselor's tone:

"The second thing is, I've decided to make Snowball my platoon sergeant. I've put him in for stripes."

The reaction was slow. Men in second squad moved quickly away; Snowball's promotion would affect them very little. The new men in first squad looked serious, but didn't really understand. Dover seemed agitated, but only because of his personal Great Cause.

Only Billy Boy's reaction was positive. He broke into applause, giving the moment an even odder turn. Okie frowned and flicked his eyes from Wolfe to Snowball, perhaps searching for collusion; Snowball licked his lips, but was silent.

"This is no reflection on you, Okie," Wolfe said, in a tone that reached for intimacy, before the dwindling group of men. "In the time I've known you I've been impressed with your leadership potential. Your time will come. But we've had that vacancy for too long, and it seems to me that Snowball, at this point in time, is the best man for the job."

Porter slapped Snowball on the back, overcoming the slight revulsion he always felt for another man's sweat. "Congratulations, Snow."

Snowball stared sadly, yet with a new face. Lifting his chin, he seemed fierce, like a recruitment poster. "Thank you, sir."

"You'll work for it," Wolfe said.

"Fuckin' lifers," Okie said, and Wolfe ignored him, like a teacher who owed one favor to his student, and now had granted it.

"Dover take the gun?" Snowball asked.

"Right," Wolfe said, assurance returning to his voice. "All right, people, let's move!"

First squad moved slowly, grievingly. Everyone liked Snowball, but this was too quick. You couldn't process it when you suspected big trouble was on its way. Stop, Porter thought. Let me off.

Dover hung back. "Sir?"

"What? What?"

"I know what you said, sir. But my old lady—"

"What's wrong with you, troop? We got a *combat mission!*"

Dover trotted off, but with his head bent, masking rage. Wolfe glared at Porter and Preacher, and they backed away. Okie walked ahead of them, arms swinging wildly.

"Is it gonna be bad, Porter?" Preacher whispered.

"I don't know. You take it slow. Watch yourself."

"I'll stay by you."

They hurried to scoop up gear, chug sodas, push rounds into chambers, grab grenades. They crawled atop the Sheridan; deep below, the driver started the engine and wheeled the turret around forward. A soldier from another tank ran up, jumped, and retrieved his shirt from the howitzer barrel. Porter squatted, slowly settling on the hot steel. Heat from the engine ebbed up.

"Fuckin' *lifers*," Okie said, almost crying.

Their destination was a numbered patch of green, a rectangular slice of jungle twenty kilometers long and twelve wide, nestled against Cambodia. There was no village near, no farm land, and everything—the tree lines, the grass—looked the same. When they'd changed directions several times, he lost his sense of north, and gave up. The tank ground onward. He scooted carefully off the hot metal, and sat on his pack.

They presented a fine target for mortars, he thought, as the two files of tanks merged, and rolled down an isthmus of grass connecting two fields. The jungle met above them, and a troupe of monkeys fled across the meshed sky, back into bamboo. Porter shifted hands on the hot grab bar, wiped away sweat, and studied the new wood lines.

They halted on the long side—west or east, he couldn't say—of the rectangle. Cherokee platoon dismounted, dropping into the grass as if into a pool, bobbing, trying to regroup amid the noise. There was a splash, a curse, someone laughing. Then they zigzagged into the woods, a zombie-like procession of floating heads. The trees were old here, unscathed by artillery, no brush beneath.

The theory was that the North Vietnamese, assuming there were any, would run from the advance of the tanks and the remaining infantry, into Cherokee's ambush. Cherokee's was possibly the safer assignment, because they could burrow down, and stick their rifles in front of their faces. Nonetheless, it seemed to Porter as if the main body was deserting them.

After Cherokee threaded into the trees, and the tanks rolled onward, Porter watched Preacher, who had his handset cupped to his ear. His face would change, should Cherokee run into an ambush before they could construct one.

In another twenty minutes the tanks had reached their entry point on the short side of the rectangle. They lined up parallel, fifteen meters apart, fifty meters from the jungle wall. Down the line Porter could see Captain Diemer and then Wolfe waving, and the infantry dropped into the grass, trying to land solidly. Snowball waded the grass between first squad's point and gun teams, yelling at the new men, "Behind the tanks!" He grinned at Porter, and Porter threw him a mock salute. Snowball turned sharply, his face fluid, as if the mock salute were truly mockery.

Porter stumbled behind the Sheridan and knelt. The ground was moist but the shoots of grass dry and brittle; he couldn't breathe, and stood again. Every engine had throttled low, awaiting word from Cherokee. Porter pointed to the radio, but Preacher shook his head. Porter removed his helmet, dropped his pack, and searched for Pall Malls.

Smoking absently, he watched the gunner atop the demolition track, twenty meters away. The man stood and ripped off his helmet. That broke his radio contact with other vehicles, a minor taboo. But briefly he was a man again, with shaggy, wet hair, and a ragged tee shirt, rather than a connection in a long circuit of weapons, jerking and firing to whispers in his ears. He stretched, and scratched his chest, as if to say, *"There.* We got here, at least." He lit a cigarette, passed it down to the hand of the driver, reaching up from inside. He took it back, said something, waited, nodded, smiled. Then he fell forward, looking puzzled. He struck his knee on a bolt head, and his face, with a quick pain, grew blank.

He was dead. So many engines ran that no one heard the shot. Nonetheless every gunner tensed, and hugged his weapon; every ear buzzed. When down the line the commander nodded, all the .50 Calibers opened up, slicing down the bamboo that began the jungle here. It dropped delicately, sifting to the ground with tall weeds and grass, as if with so many rounds it was momentarily suspended. The firing was vengeful, more sustained and disciplined than the firing at the crane had been. It was pride, and nothing could withstand it.

Behind them all, a detail sliced grass with machetes, to establish an aid station. The medical track withdrew, and dropped its tailgate. Two men carried out tables.

Cherokee radioed that they'd established their ambush. Two Sheridans, neither of them Porter's, rumbled forward for the point, and the other tanks moved laboriously into files behind them. Snowball spread his men between the files—as did all the platoon leaders.

There was a deeper rumble, like an unexpected chord in a piece of music, and then a quaking light. Porter looked up as rain gently fell, the sun reflected in it still. He realized that he hadn't looked up since Jolly Green dropped from the sky. The rain might present a problem, but for now it cooled him, and offered a brief serenity. The tanks steamed and seemed to run more quietly, as if they drank rain.

The tanks leaned up against, and then uprooted, trees eight inches in diameter. Bamboo splintered and fell like wheat before combines, but then became a mat underneath, of arched and springing branches, and little ankle-traps. Preacher fell, and ripped his pants at the knee.

Smoking another Pall Mall, Porter stared into a jungle that with the rain seemed darker, and murkier. He saw Captain Diemer, atop the command tank, speaking into a handset carried by a man Porter didn't know. Johnson, Diemer's previous RTO, had left two weeks before for a supply job in Tay Ninh. Porter lobbied hard for Johnson's old job, but Wolfe blocked his candidacy, telling

Diemer that Porter was a born point man.

So late in his tour, Porter understood he'd never find a job in the rear. He liked Captain Diemer, but hardly knew him. He was where he'd started: nothing much learned, near to death as ever. Just now it didn't matter. Officer or enlisted, black or white, soon they'd all be equal.

Small arms fire broke out a long way ahead. Porter glanced toward Preacher, who nodded. "They're running into Cherokee."

"Maybe we won't have to go all the way in," a new man said.

"Not a chance," Okie said, stepping out ahead.

Snowball danced about, trying to keep the squad dispersed should mortars begin; he walked back to confer with Wolfe, who managed second squad. Dover and Billy Boy stood a distance apart: Dover talked, and Billy Boy giggled.

Heavy fire opened up on the right. From behind a shield, his body half out of the hole that dropped into the machine itself, the gunner atop the right point tank returned fire, until his barrel steamed. First squad threw out grenades, and dropped to the splintery ground. Smoke drifted back and clung like fog. The gunner resumed his firing, and Wolfe ordered the entire platoon out to the flank. Porter crouched, trying to make out something to shoot at.

Now the gunner fired with one hand, his free arm twisting in the air like a bull rider's. His tank wheeled beneath him to advance, and then there was a deep, muffled explosion, and a clot of smoke, as the tank hit a mine. Part of a tread flew back and landed in the middle of first squad— flying slow enough to dodge. One side of the tank lifted off the ground, and when it fell again the gunner bucked up high. He came down dead, and then a rocket sailed in and exploded below his neck. The head and chest disappeared.

Firing from the nearby tanks stopped abruptly, with men shouting, and smoke everywhere. Far back in the right column, Diemer stood, screamed something, and pointed to the sky. A jet's coming in, Porter thought. He crawled backward, one hand bleeding from the bamboo, marveling that Diemer would stand so tall in the middle of a firefight. He reached for another Pall Mall, but the pack was sodden—no time to dig in his gear.

"Man hurt!" Billy Boy shouted, "Hurt, hurt! Man hurt!"

There were two neat small holes above Dover's wrist. Beside him, Billy Boy poked into the crushed bamboo with his rifle barrel, and looked grim. Snowball and Wolfe came quickly.

"Let's see," Wolfe said. He glanced around as the squad grouped. "Don't bunch up, men."

"Fuck," said Okie. "He ain't hurt. It's just—"

Billy Boy knelt, and propped Dover up. "You gonna be awright, Dove?"

"Oh," Dover said faintly. "It hurts."

"Sure, Dove."

Okie spat. "He done that himself, Lieutenant."

"I *saw* it," Billy Boy said indignantly, pointing down at the bamboo. "I *saw* it."

"Snake," Porter murmured, only now understanding.

"Maybe it wasn't poisonous," Wolfe said hopefully. He looked anxiously in the direction of Diemer, than at Snowball. As he began to speak the jet made its first pass, dropping two five hundred pounders with a clunk and fiery crashing. Debris settled with the rain. "What you think, Sergeant?" Wolfe asked, his voice punctuated by a burst of AK fire that began before the jet was quite up the sky again.

"No snake at all," Okie insisted.

"Cain't be *sure,* babes," said Snowball. He knelt. "You shammin' it, Dove?"

"Oh, Lord," Dover moaned. "Oh, please, please . . . "

Wolfe stepped past Dover, moving toward Diemer, who motioned from the command tank. "I—don't—know," he said, his voice cut up by small arms. "Get two men, Snow—two of the new men. Carry him to the field."

"You'll be okay, Dove," said Billy Boy.

Dover moaned. The jet pounced again, strafing; the empty shell casings pattered through the leaves overhead like little bombs. Porter and Okie watched as the jet veered up again, while two of the new men, straining to conceal their delight, carried Dover toward the field.

"I'd a fixed his black ass," Okie said. "I'd a put him up on the point. You hear Snow? Those bastards stick together. Just because he cain't wait to go on R. & R. like anybody else."

Porter shrugged.

Okie bent and stuck his hand into the bamboo. "Snake," he said. "Nice snake. Here, snake."

Porter glimpsed the belly of Jolly Green's bird, a dull green above the treetops, one landing light flashing. More AK fire, and the bird lifted sharply from sight.

A burst of machine gun fire ripped across the demolition track. Shortly, as smoke poured from within, the crew climbed up, and leaped off. Coils of white detonator cord came alive, extended, snapped in the air like electric arcs. A man still on top blew to the ground, and hunched along painfully, his shirt soaked in blood. Rocking with explosions, puffs of smoke rolling from every hole, the track plowed into the bamboo, stalled, died, then burned in earnest.

Ahead, the disabled point tank looked like some blind, green, prehistoric beast as the driver tried to maneuver out of the way of the columns behind, only to hit another mine. Steam hissed. A fountain of coolant shot up, spraying the stump of the dead man. The driver gave up at last, and ran to another tank.

The second platoon had moved up, mixing with Porter's, and now he could hear Diemer and the tank commander above him. "He what?" said the commander.

"He says link up. Link up. My Cherokee platoon's running out of ammo."

"I can't move. Nobody said they had *mines,* Mister. I got nine men dead and three tracks down. Link up? Fucking Pie in the Sky."

Diemer dipped his forehead into a palm, pinched his temples with a thumb and forefinger. The muscles in his arm flexed. "They're gonna get chewed up," he said. "They're gonna get chewed up."

"Can't move! Except *back*. Outta here." Wolfe looked meaningfully at Porter, and Porter stepped back, understanding that all of this was not for his ears. Then he heard Wolfe say, "I'll go in, sir. We'll get through."

He was volunteering!

Diemer shook his head—not, Porter thought, in refusal, but with an inability to consider. The battalion radio crackled with Jolly Green's voice and Diemer reached for the handset, like someone who was already on the phone.

Porter joined Preacher, and spun him around to switch the radio to the battalion frequency. Preacher held the handset so they both could hear: ". . . Gooks not more than one zero zero meters east your point vehicle. Plain as day up here. Running into your ambush element. But link up! Link up! I say again: you *must* link up. Cherokee has a body count of two-six, were you aware?"

"Negative," said Diemer.

"You're kickin' ass, pardner! Get your patrol up there; we got 'em nailed. We'll run some interference up here, so sit tight zero-four, then move when the shit lifts. How copy?"

"Solid copy."

"Jolly Green, out."

"What is it, Porter?" Preacher asked.

Porter switched back to the company frequency. "It's us. We're up."

A Cobra gunship dove, firing rockets that trailed plumes of purple smoke. Two jets came screeching.

Snowball approached, looking guilty. His eyes rose mournfully, and when they met Porter's, leapt with surprise. He stared between the columns of tanks. "You got to point, Porter."

"Right," Porter said, and picked up his rifle.

Preacher stepped near. "I wish you were a Christian, Porter."

Porter opened his mouth to reply, but found no words.

It was almost quiet: engines behind them, idling low, and rain soft as thought. Only a little firing came from Cherokee's direction.

A brightly-colored bird flew up in his face; he jerked back, and brushed the water from his eyes with a wet sleeve. He crouched, trying to see what lay ahead, and fighting off an uneasiness in his stomach that was not quite nausea. He hadn't realized how near dark it was.

They might be waiting until three or four of the platoon passed—they'd aim at Preacher because of his antenna, or Snowball because he was black. They disliked black skin.

One thing: they'd had no time to set booby traps.

He moved forward another fifteen meters, crouching a little, turning his head left and right. Now he saw the barest indication of a path, a sort of tunnel through the foliage. In five more steps he discovered a sandal imprint, melting in the rain. Enough of hunches: they were here still, one at least, not a minute ahead. With a flooded eye he traced a line forward, trying to establish that shadows weren't bodies. Perhaps the man was wounded, running like a gut shot deer . . . there was a burst of fire ahead, possibly confirming the enemy soldier's presence, or his death. Porter spotted three small stumps, sawed off evenly. He didn't want to go any farther.

Okie slipped to his side. "There," Porter murmured, pointing toward the stumps. "That'll be the bunker complex. You see that footprint?"

"Yeah." Okie nodded. "Be an observation bunker maybe fifty feet. He might be in there." He pivoted on his toes, and motioned to Snowball. He gestured left and right: a new man and Billy Boy took positions looking out.

Snowball brought the machine gun down from his shoulder. "Know where they be?"

"Where they *might* be," Okie whispered, motioning.

Porter could barely see, and he was cold. He heard shouts a good distance behind, a deep groaning as the tanks turned around. Firing had ceased. The smoke had washed away. It was time to go: drink coffee, smoke Pall Malls, read perfumed letters.

"Bring in some artillery?" Snowball asked.

"Don't much want to," Porter said. "With dark comin' on. We don't know for sure where Cherokee is. We can't be that precise."

"No, no," Preacher said, pointing at his handset. "They got out the back way. Tanks already went after 'em."

Snowball looked grave. "Where's Jolly Green?"

"Headed for Tay Ninh. Said he wasn't gonna fly around in the pourin' rain if we was done killin' bad guys."

"Back at the mess hall," Porter said. "Eatin' ice cream with strawberries on top."

"Shit an' shinola," Okie said. "Let's head on back. Get somethin' to eat. Snow?"

Snowball shook his head. "We cain't, babes. Lieutenant Wolfe say we turn around, we turn around. You go on, Porter."

Porter couldn't believe it. "'Go *on*, Porter?'"

"You go on."

"Jesus H. Christ! I got sixty-three days. I don't have to listen to this shit. You goddam . . . *coon!*"

"Porter!" said Snowball. "You—"

"You blackassed lifer. What the hell you—"

"Shut up, Porter," Okie said. "You cain't talk like that. Hush!"

"Lay off me, motherfucker!"

Preacher tapped Porter's shoulder. "No," he said. "Porter. No. No."

Porter turned his face into the rain. He heard them rustling confusedly behind. At length Okie squatted nearby, began to speak—but didn't. Porter found a dry Pall Mall, but a raindrop hit it, and he threw it angrily away. Okie passed him his Camel; Porter cupped it carefully, and took several long drags. He glanced over his shoulder, avoiding Snowball's eyes.

Wolfe bent near. "What's the problem, Porter?"

"It's almost dark. We're walkin' into bunkers."

"Cherokee killed a lot of gooks. What did you expect?"

"I saw a sandal imprint. It's fresh. In this rain? I'm not goin' anywhere."

"I been thinkin', sir," Okie cut in. "Cherokee done got out; don't seem to be any reason to be *on* this patrol. Reckon we'll go on back?"

Wolfe bent his head, as if amused, and lit a cigarette beneath the bevel of his helmet. When he looked up, it was through a wreath of smoke. "We have our orders. I'd like to go a little farther."

"You could call up Captain Diemer, sir," Okie said. "It's rainin'—almost dark. Anybody up there—ain't sayin' there *is*—Porter's right, they got us by the balls. Come back in the mornin', sir. The whole company, tanks behind us, lotsa sunshine."

Wolfe nodded as if he agreed, but turned to Snowball. "How about it, Sergeant?"

Droplets of rain slid off Snowball's face in the waning light, and seemed silvery. He stared at Porter steadily. "Maybe one or two gooks."

Wolfe grasped Porter's shoulder. He tilted his head, and smiled, like an indulgent father. "What say, point man? Let's go a little farther, shall we?"

"It's suicide."

The lieutenant shook his head, still seemingly amused. "I don't think so, Porter. I think Cherokee drove them off, and we'll just run a little inventory while their shit is weak. Get any documents they left before they can come back, you know, at 0200. All right?"

"Nosir. I'm not going any direction but backwards. I can't see. The mission is *over*. Maybe *you'd* like to point into those bunkers . . . *sir*."

Wolfe lowered his head again, and released a long breath. Cigarette smoke hung on his face like a beard. His eyes were only dark spaces. "You know that's not my function, Porter."

"What *is* your function?" Porter lifted his head. "To get me killed? I'm sick of this teamwork crap, if I gotta be the goddam football."

It was quiet. The insistent rain, the quickening darkness, shrouded them all. Preacher's face bent near—incredulous, terrified.

The lieutenant rose. He cast his cigarette away. "All right, Porter. I'll point."

<<>>

This was not what Porter wanted. He had no interest in defiance. He wanted someone to say, "You're right. Of course, you're right." Now he felt robbed even of his minor status as a point man, and would gladly have shared in the lunacy. He wanted to run from behind, and take charge.

Officers didn't take the point. It was the law.

But Wolfe was careful. He held his rifle as if it might shatter in his hands, and took new steps only after eying every dark leaf. He motioned to Okie, and whispered.

At last he reached the observation bunker. A shadowy arm lay atop it, at first seeming like a fallen branch. Wolfe kicked it away, dropped to the mud, and snaked over the bunker's roof. He held up a grenade and looked back at Porter—or so it seemed. Faces no longer had expressions. Wolfe dropped the grenade through a firing portal, and the muffled explosion took Porter back, to a sunny day when he'd thrown a cherry bomb into the cistern. Even now he was eight years old, with his mother scolding him.

Wolfe stood, and studied the dark buildings of the bunker complex. He motioned, and the men moved silently around him, fanning in a semicircle. Porter made out bags of rice beneath a shed, cutting tools, broken weapons. In an open-air kitchen, coals spluttered, and briefly winked bright. Snowball brushed past with his machine gun, and Porter moved near him. He struggled for a way to apologize.

"Spread out along the edge," whispered Wolfe roughly, the beginning of a cold bubbling in his throat. "Okie, Billy Boy, when they get in position, check for documents and weapons. Preacher, let me have that radio."

Porter remained by Snowball. Once more he tried to speak, and couldn't. Unbelievably, Billy Boy paused to compliment Wolfe on his job of pointing; the lieutenant waved him away. Holding Preacher's handset, with Preacher shivering at his side, Wolfe spoke to Porter across the dark space: "I'll bust you."

"I know it, sir."

Wolfe shook his head. "I thought you were born to point. No nerves. I thought you loved it."

Porter had filled with grief. "No, sir. How could anybody—?"

Wolfe brought up the handset, and his lips parted, probably to answer the captain. It seemed anticlimactic, a terrible cheat after all their caution. Three rounds popped out of the rain. Wolfe fell, and died.

Six more rounds popped out of the rain. A new men dropped, and Preacher died with a gurgle. Porter took two steps forward. Had it happened?

"Down! Down! Down!" screamed Okie.

Snowball jumped behind the gun. Porter lay beside him, and fed ammo. Snowball fired forty rounds, spraying wildly. Bags of rice split open, and peppered them. The belt grew short.

"Ammo! Ammo!" Porter yelled back, and two

boxes thudded at his feet. He reached back for them, and they were slick with mud, like flour paste, or grease, or blood. He snapped on a fresh belt, but Snowball lay still.

"Snow," Porter said. "Snow."

Porter rolled him over. He bled at the neck. Though his eyes were open, they were dark as the night, and Porter couldn't read them. "Snow?" He didn't know if Snowball saw him. "Snow?" Porter could have sworn that Snowball had gone pale. Pale as a . . . ghost.

"The tree!" Okie yelled, from somewhere ahead. "The fuckin' tree!"

But Porter couldn't move. He knew which tree Okie meant, and he realized that a man was firing from there. The man *would* fire at the gun. It made sense, he thought, as Snowball bled on him.

Clawing at bodies, Billy Boy leaped in beside him, and pushed Snowball aside. He tilted the gun toward the tree. On and on Billy Boy fired.

"Feed it!" Okie screamed. "Porter, Porter, feed it!" So he did, clipping on another belt.

Something fell.

"Hold it! Hold on," Okie said. He stood, a skinny shadow creeping near.

Billy Boy kept firing.

"Stop it," Porter said. "Stop."

Billy Boy kept firing. Porter yanked at the belt, and the gun jammed. "Billy Boy," Porter said.

Billy Boy shook all over.

Porter crawled into the personnel carrier as if

into a cave. The gate whined up and he couldn't see anything but the glow of the driver's cigarette. Tins of food rolled on the floor, and water splashed against his boots. Everything smelled like diesel fuel.

They couldn't see, the blood made him slippery, and so it was impossible to hold him still. When they hit a log, his head lurched into Porter's ribs. He shifted hands, wiped the free hand on his shirt. Once, he thought, Snowball gasped. "That driver—"

"Cain't see," Okie said. "He cain't see."

"I wish we could get him level."

Snowball's body heaved—or it was the carrier again, dropping into a hole. "Goin' home, Snow," Porter said.

"Walkin' down the street," Okie said. "Pretty girls everywhere."

"You just stay awake, Snow," Porter said. "You hear me?

They reached the field, though Porter didn't know this until the gate whined down. They crawled out in the rain, and Snowball kept slipping away. Exhausted, they lowered him onto the wet grass. Things seemed better then, with Snowball on the ground, and their hands free.

But it seemed like the wrong place. It seemed like the end of someone else's battle. Lights criss-crossed, blinding Porter. He didn't know where Dover and Billy Boy were.

Finally, a man came toward them, juggling a powerful light. It played off the treetops, and plunged deep into the jungle. Porter saw a path diving jaggedly into darkness, but did not believe he'd come from there.

The medic bent low with his light. "I'm sorry," he said. "This soldier's dead."

Around the perimeter the armored and infantry parted, as though there were shame in each other's company. The armored fired up their tapes of Hendrix and the Doors and disappeared inside the tracks. The infantry withdrew to the very center, and made a circle of its own.

A brand-new lieutenant, who'd flown out on the mail bird, came slogging through the mud to ask for the tank commander, but no one seemed to know where he was. The lieutenant tried to talk to Captain Diemer, but Diemer wouldn't answer. Finally the lieutenant withdrew. He hung near various groups, and moved on again, unnoticed.

Diemer was on the battalion radio for a long time. His voice was all you heard as you tried to eat or read a letter. He seemed shaky and self-conscious, as though he were auditioning for a school play. Occasionally, he grew angry.

He meant to call in the names of the dead, but Battalion was too far away, and perhaps also the faltering rain interfered. "Say again," a voice at Battalion replied, clearly. "Read you weak and distorted." The captain repeated the men's names. "Say again," said Battalion, down a river of static. "Say again."

Joint after joint went around but it had no effect on Porter. He didn't float away, or grow sleepy. He stalked the perimeter, rubbing his neck. He ran into Okie. Okie handed him a perfumed letter, but they didn't speak. Porter tucked the letter away and forgot about it.

There was a surprise. The armored cook had made a great pot of bean soup, and put out a slab of Wisconsin cheddar cheese. Porter cut a piece of the cheese, grabbed some bread, and stuffed it all inside his shirt. He forgot about the cheese but continued walking the perimeter, sipping the wonderful soup, smoking Pall Malls, staring into men's faces.

Someone told him that Dover was dead. How? Was there really a snake?

"They run right at me," Billy Boy said. "I told Shari, I said I wasn't ever gonna shoot nobody." He began to giggle, and everyone grew silent. Billy Boy spun around, holding an imaginary machine gun. "Eh-eh-eh-eh!" he said. *"Got 'em."*

"Hush, now," said Okie.

"Eh-eh-eh-eh-eh! This foot comes back at me?" Billy Boy kept giggling. The light from a diesel candle fluttered over his face. "It was still in the boot, like. Laced up? Isn't that weird? They just kept comin'—"

Okie grabbed him. Billy Boy tried to fight, and swung his arms wildly. One of the new men, still a stranger to Porter, stepped in front of Billy Boy and slapped his face repeatedly, hard. Billy Boy slipped from Okie's arms down into the grass. "Oh oh oh," he said.

"Christ," Okie said to the new man. "What you do that for? This ain't the fuckin' movies, troop."

Lightning quaked on the horizon. The rain turned to mist, and stopped, but the moon never came out. Porter wrapped his poncho liner tightly around him, like a bandage. It had stayed dry. He lay down and pulled his poncho over his head. Then he remembered his cheese and bread, and munched on it deep down under, where no one could see him. When he opened his eyes the sun was shining, and the cheese lay by his hand.

Where They Have to Take You in

IT WAS CHRISTMAS DAY and Oklahoma City was shut up tight. A wind gusted from the northwest, blowing paper cups and an occasional tumbleweed across the abandoned streets. It was beginning to snow.

All Andy Bright wore to combat the cold was a Taiwanese windbreaker and a ragged stocking cap he'd found at a telephone booth inside the airport, when he was trying to dial the old man. So he dropped his duffel bag and dug toward the bottom, past fatigue shirts and the olive drab boxer shorts he'd never worn, and his Nikon camera he'd bought at the PX in Ton Son Nhut, and the Hell's Angels kimono a boom-boom girl in Vung Tao had given him—and his boots, of course, colored red from the clay along that creek at Tay Ninh. That bloody creek.

Finally, he pulled out the heavy coat they'd issued him at Ft. Campbell, and that he'd dragged to Seattle and Saigon and now back again. The duffel bag weighed less and it felt good to be walking up Meridian in the middle of Oklahoma, not drawing stares as he had in San Francisco.

Maybe he didn't want to go to Alva. He'd buy a car and drive down to Nuevo Laredo, get filthy drunk, rent a whore for a week. Mosey on to Ft. Carson when his cash was gone. Wasn't that the army way?

He knew he couldn't live with his father. The other men heard from their wives, their sweethearts, their sisters, their ministers, their kid brothers, their fucking maiden aunts. Nobody wrote to Andy. A month before, he'd dropped a note he'd be home around Christmas. No reply. In the thirty-six hours he'd been stateside, he'd tried five times to call. No answer.

There was little traffic on Meridian. But, one after the other, three women in red dresses drove by, and each smiled. The last even waved, and so it couldn't be true that everybody hated soldiers. He waved back, speculating that the woman would stop and he could talk her into driving him to Alva. Wasn't that fair? After a year in Vietnam?

At the Oakland terminal he'd watched two hippies make a point of spitting on a chaplain. Put your life on the line and that was the treatment you got.

Of course, he didn't have much use for chaplains himself. You stood out on some airstrip while they mumbled over the bodies. If you went to one with a problem he'd try to get you to re-enlist. But the hippies were spitting on a symbol, not somebody real.

"Spit on me!" Andy shouted to the cold wind. "I'll take you out."

He detoured for a Salvation Army drop box, where he left the boxer shorts, the Hell's Angels kimono, and the Air France bag packed with the mildewed civvies he'd bought in Hong Kong. He stepped into a gas station, the first place he'd seen that was open, and stood over the register, rubbing his hands. Three days before, he lay on a bunk in Bien Hoa, sweating so much the sheets were wet.

The boy behind the counter wasn't any older than Andy. "You in the Nam?"

Andy poured himself coffee. "Just gettin' home."

"You kill anybody over there?"

"I killed somebody nearly every day. I killed people for breakfast." Andy put coffee, a Mr. Goodbar, and a pair of mason's gloves on the counter. "I want those Garcia y Vegas," he said, pointing.

"You can just have the coffee," the boy said. "But I got to charge you for the rest. Didn't you have someone to meet you?"

"Naw." Andy looked at the floor. "Came in kinda sudden."

The boy reached under the counter and produced a picture of a blonde in a swimsuit. "That's my girl. Carrie."

Andy smiled crookedly. "I forgot what they

look like."

There were more red women at the Nazarene college, huddling outside the chapel. They all were so pretty and had such pretty legs. "I'm a leg-man!" Andy shouted, but the women ignored him. Andy wanted to be properly introduced to that redhead, say, and he'd go to church with her, and study hard at her school. Afterwards, he'd find a job where he wore a tie.

Maybe not. His mother, who was Assembly of God, had not spoken well of Nazarenes.

He went into a phone booth and dialed Alva again, but it was useless. He charged toward the women, yelling "Shit!" to see what they'd do. They scurried into the church except for one, a woman bigger than Andy. She ran toward him shouting about how he profaned the holy day.

"Okay, okay," he said, backpedaling.

He hadn't meant anything. He was having some fun. He was full of energy and wanted to run, and scream, and get laid.

He walked up Rockwell toward Oklahoma 3. "Fuck 'em if they cain't take a joke," he muttered. They didn't know what he'd been through. He almost wished he was back in the unit. Half the time you just lay around, smoked dope, and played the guitar. Andy could play all the Creedence songs, and he could sing, too.

He was at the city limits now, where the beautiful homes were more widely dispersed, and trailers popped up in the scrub oak. He lit a cigar and marched up the cracked asphalt, and at the top of the hill he could see for fifty miles. Not quite the Midwest, not quite the West. Oak and pine and sagebrush, here and there a yucca plant, red rock bluffs in the distance rising out of the white flats. There were only a few towns, and you had to look hard even to spot a cow.

His ears were freezing. He rubbed them and walked backwards so the snow would hit him a different way. And this time when he turned a state trooper sat beckoning, in a big white Plymouth coated with alkali. "You fightin' a war out here, young sergeant?"

"Nosir."

"I think you been to a certain Asian nation. What was your MOS?"

"Eleven Bravo, sir. I was infantry all the way. First Cav!"

"Is that the outfit—is that the *same* outfit—that got its tail whipped in Ko-rea?"

"I don't know nothin' about that, sir."

"I had a complaint about you. These nice Christian women, they said you was staggerin' around like a drunk rapist."

"I ain't nothin' like that, sir. There wasn't nothing open in the city and I couldn't get through on the phone."

The trooper pulled at an eyelid. He was an old man. "I was in France in World War II."

"Was that pretty rough, sir?"

"I was with Patton. We seen some heavy fightin', but we didn't piss and moan, and we sure as hell didn't take no drugs."

"I never smoked dope when I was in Vietnam. Nosir."

"So where you walkin' to, young sergeant?"

"Alva."

"Two hundred miles!" The officer shook his head sadly. "I don't walk anywheres since the state of Oklahoma give me this car. It's warm in this car. It's got a damn fine heater."

"I never meant to scare those ladies. I was walkin' there, that's all. I just wanted to say hello to somebody."

"Climb in, son."

"Sir?"

"I reckon it's Alva or bust."

Andy stood on the darkened porch, watching snow swirl in the streetlamps. He pulled out the house key he'd carried through the war, on a chain with his P-38 can opener and a whistle his mother had for supervising playground at the church school. There had been times when he couldn't remember what the key was for, but he was always comforted by the whistle.

The door was unlocked. "Hello?" he said. "Daddy?" He threw the duffel bag into his room and stalked through the house. The place was neater than his father usually kept it, and, for a moment, he thought the house had sold, that he was intruding upon strangers. No, there was the photograph of his great grandfather's orchard in Maryland, and now the Kelvinator came on with the same squawk that scared him when he was a little kid.

I'm the same, he said to himself. I'm all right.

He turned on the TV and saw a formation of helicopters, flying Christmas dinner to the troops. There was a shot of a grunt with a paper plateful of turkey, mashed potatoes, and gravy. The jungle looked like home.

He opened the refrigerator, but was so weary he couldn't focus on making a sandwich. There was a jar of pickles that had been there when he went off to basic training. He sniffed the jar and threw it angrily into the trash. He sliced off a chunk of cheddar and went into his room, where an F-4 Phantom dangled from the ceiling. Tenth grade? "Huh," he murmured, and collapsed across the bed.

He woke to a gust of wind rattling the window where, during the summers, he used to sit with his .22, waiting for the rabbits that came out of the woods and stood an instant, ears cocked and nostrils wrinkling, before they invaded the vegetable garden. Now, the woods were silent under the snow. It was almost dark. He heard the clock in the living room hiss and strike six times.

A light went on in the kitchen and he almost called out, "Daddy!" Then a woman crossed the doorway toward the stove and returned with a saucepan. She sat at the table, reading from a paperback romance, eating out of the saucepan.

She kicked off her shoes, and, with a sudden gesture, hunched up in the chair to pull down her stockings.

He lay contemplating her bare legs, hoping that she'd turn so he'd see more, because, if this was his father's girlfriend, the old man had done well. Then Andy was anxious. Which was better: to turn over, pretend to sleep, and let her discover him, or to march in and say hello?

He slipped across the hall and stood in the doorway. "Ma'am—"

She dropped the saucepan to the floor, scattering little pieces of spaghetti. She scooted back, nearly tipping over in her chair, catching herself with a hand.

"Hey! I'm Andy. I'm—"

"I knew . . . I *know*. You never called!"

"I did. Yes, ma'am, I sure tried to."

Her breasts heaved. "You really scared me." She forced a smile. "I . . . had to work today, I wasn't here." She sighed. "Welcome home, Andy! Your father is in New Jersey."

"You're—"

"Mavis. Your father's . . . well, we're engaged. I don't *live* here—I wouldn't, I wouldn't just *live* with a man. George and I are planning to get married in the spring. This house—*your* house—is close to work, and sometimes—"

She was a waitress at the Kanoke, and Christmas Day, plopping down canned turkey for every lonely guy in town, had been frantic. But she offered to fix him something to eat.

"I can cook," he said, moving to the stove, smiling at her. "Let me fix *you* something."

"I'll just sit here and have a cigarette." He held out his Zippo and she lit a Marlboro, meeting his eyes as she released smoke. "It's not a good witness for the Lord, is it? But I don't smoke, not really. I get nervous. You scared me." She smashed the cigarette and lit another. "You know, your father won't even heat up soup."

He shrugged. "When I was in high school I did it all. Did the laundry."

"After your mother died, you mean. You all had a struggle, didn't you? So what are your plans, Andy?"

"Thought maybe I'd go to college."

"Here?"

"Sure. Only I still got five months in the army up in Colorado."

She put her hand on his arm. "I'm sorry you had to go through all that. That awful war."

He lowered his head nobly, but, for the moment, his cheeseburger and lima beans were compensation enough for his sufferings. He spread mustard on the burger and melted a patty of margarine on the beans. "You get ham and lima beans in C-rations. Everybody hated 'em, only I thought they tasted just like a dish my mom used to make." He took another bite. "So how did you and Daddy get together?"

"He came to the Kanoke real early for break-

breakfast. Five o'clock, even before the ranchers are out. He'd drink three cups of coffee and sit there, staring at the paper, like he was tryin' to work up his nerve to climb in that truck again. Like it took courage, you know what I mean?

"Well, I could see it on his face he was hurtin' bad, he was full of grief. But I knew he liked me, so I started talkin' to him. You know it's hard for the folks that stay at home, too."

"He ever mention me?"

"He said you were in combat and he hoped you didn't get wounded."

Andy reached for Mavis's cigarettes. "It was real fucked up."

She blinked. "This is your home, Andy, but I'd appreciate it if you restrained your language."

"It was *bad*. All the guys on drugs and the black dudes, they wanted to kill you just for breathin'. We all knew it was a load of crap." He stared intently. She smoked but she was a Bible-thumper. It confounded his understanding of the world. "And this chaplain—this is an awful thing, Mavis."

"Go ahead."

"Some hippy came up and spit on him there in Oakland. A chaplain." He stared at her meaning-fully. "A *chaplain*."

"That's a terrible thing for anybody to see. But you're home now, Andy. You have your whole life ahead of you."

"You got a car? Let's go get some ice cream."

She turned her eyes. "I'm worn out. I'm not fixed up."

"You look fine." Andy grinned. "The old man did good."

She dug in her purse for keys. "You go. I think Metzger's is open."

He bought three quarts of ice cream and a six-pack of Coor's, putting the ice cream in the trunk where it would stay frozen. Mavis's car was a 1964 Galaxy, an automatic with a 289 V-8. It had a good heater and a radio that pulled in the national band of Vietnam, Creedence Clearwater Revival. He cruised the square once, singing, "Suzi-Q," but nothing was open and there were no other cars. So he headed southwest, down U.S. 281 toward the sandy, crossroads town of Waynoka, just for the feeling of a car on the road.

He pulled into a driveway to turn around, and popped another beer. His headlights were trained on someone's porch. He'd wait until they came to the door, then roar away.

Something he used to do, when he was young and stupid.

Then he realized that he was staring at bales of hay—that the house was being used for a barn. He cut the engine, and one marooned cow bawled in the moonlight. His boots crunched on the snow as he walked up the lane. He drained the beer, threw the bottle at the house, and it hit the shake roof and sailed away. He urinated on a fence post, shook like a dog, and walked back to the Ford. Jesus, it was cold.

He opened another beer and pointed the big car toward Alva again, thinking, a man could get a little place like that cheap. Fix up the house. He had some money saved, since there had been no way to spend it. But what would he do with his own place? Run a few cattle. Get drunk every night.

Maybe grow some marijuana.

His headlights dropped on Northwest Oklahoma State, where half his high school class had gone. He parked and walked by the stores, studying the windows full of sports jackets and short skirts.

Books, too. He'd done some reading in the army. Not just fuckbooks, but some Robert Heinlein, and all about the little Hobbits and Bilbo Baggins. And *Portnoy's Complaint,* though, come to think of it, that was sort of a fuckbook. Anyhow, he could fit in. It wasn't branded on his forehead that he'd been in Vietnam.

He sat on a bench and blew smoke at the moon. He liked sitting between the tall buildings, spying on learning. If he'd been smarter he'd have enrolled, too, and avoided the war. "It was the thing to do," he said aloud. "It seemed like the ting to do!"

They'd pay him to go to school now. He walked under the big cottonwoods and shuffled through the snow across a street that didn't go through. A car whipped around the corner below and caught Andy in its headlights.

He froze, then ran. Why am I running? he asked himself, and stopped. *I don't have to run.* He caught his breath, looked back. Two men got out of the car and pointed their flashlights. Security!

He ran between two brick buildings with high, ornate windows, and turned sharply. Under the windows of the building to his right were a row of holly bushes, trimmed like hedge. He crawled behind the holly, flush to the brick. He scooped up snow and leaves and burrowed down. His heart was pounding so loudly he wondered if it could be heard. Now the men turned the corner, casting about their lights.

"You see him?"

"Maybe went down the hill."

"You see him?"

"Some Mexican." Casually, the man played his light over the holly and onto the wall above Andy.

The men walked on.

Andy crawled out and went the other way, feeling scared and foolish. He liked how he felt, too. They hadn't found him! He ran across the campus and onto 281, where he'd parked the car. He drove carefully to his father's house.

He took the last of the beers and crept into his bedroom, where he turned on the TV. *It's a Wonderful Life* was showing.

Mavis came to his doorway. "I was worried about you."

"I took a little drive. There's some ice cream in the refrigerator."

She padded off and returned with a dish of rocky road. "I shouldn't eat this," she said. "I don't need the calories."

"Oh, you're a good-looking woman, Mavis."

"Anything would look good to you."

"That's not so. You're a very nice lady. Come sit with me."

"I cain't."

"Pretty, pretty please. I get bad dreams from all the horrors of combat I experienced." He wriggled under the covers. "Come tuck me in!"

Frowning, she pulled the bedclothes up and slid a pillow under his head. "Whoo," she said. "You smell like a still."

"Good night, Mommy," he said, but she didn't laugh.

He ordered bacon and eggs at the Skelly truckstop and then sat slumped at the counter, his face wreathed in cigarette smoke, his eyes on the ass of a good-looking blonde. She went off-shift and stalked past him theatrically, buttoned her coat at the door, never once met his eyes. She got into her car, a Barracuda two-door with a piece torn out of the grill and fuzzy dice hanging from the rearview mirror, and then through the plate glass he saw her smile. He smiled back.

The rancher beside Andy yanked on the bill of his cap and laughed. Andy stood and strode for the cash register. The owner, a gray-haired woman, peered down through her bifocals.

"You're Andy, aren't you?"

"Yes, ma'am."

"You used to come in here with your dad for a lemon-lime. Then you went off to Vietnam."

The rancher grabbed a toothpick. "We ain't gonna win that thing. We don't *wanta* win it."

"Will you be settlin' down now, Andy?"

"Goin' to college."

"Very good." She scribbled a number on the back of Andy's receipt. "My advice to you with Lindsey is try her on a Thursday. She takes Fridays and Saturdays off."

The rancher grinned. "How come you never give me no advice like that, Boo-Boo?"

"You call me Boo-Boo one more time, Bob, and I will reach under this counter, pull out my Colt .45, and blow your head off."

"Love," the rancher said, winking at Andy. "Ain't it grand?"

At the drugstore Andy bought two Robert Heinlein novels and, also, *Atlas Shrugged,* because there was a guy in his unit, Gordie Haskell, who talked about Ayn Rand. Gordie the Good, everyone called him, because he'd always share his water, or loan you money. Gordie was killed sitting on the green line one night. There were five of them on top of the bunker, looking at the stars, and Gordie was talking about Ayn Rand. Suddenly, he fell over, a bullet through his heart.

Andy walked along Flint Creek, where chunks of ice floated, and steam rose. He remembered the creek from when he was a kid and looked for terrapins there.

He was feeling good. He had books to read and money in his pockets. He hadn't been wounded, that was the main thing. Maybe he would think about Gordie for a long time, but Gordie was dead and Andy stood erect, finished with war, a free man.

And there was Lindsey. What did he have to lose? He could spend all his money on her and it wouldn't matter. He could promise her anything and it wouldn't matter. No way around it, he had to go to Colorado.

He was still walking by the creek when he saw the car, and just looking at it gave him power. On the corner lot where the Sinclair station used to be, covered with red dust and grimy snow, was a 1955 Chevrolet.

He signed his name and counted out his money to a man in a red sports coat named Frank. Then he was off for the red rock country to the west, down between giant boulders by the wide Canadian River, into the Oklahoma sunset that burned across the snow.

Mavis stood out front in her best, but it wasn't as though she'd been waiting for him. She stared as if he'd landed from Mars, or at least from Kansas. His engine rumbled low.

"It's a real cute car, Andy. Take me to church?"

"I ain't got no clothes."

"It's just prayer meeting, it don't matter."

He revved the motor. She slid along the plastic seat cover with a rude squeak, tilting her legs toward him, straightening them and pulling at her skirt.

Suddenly, there was nothing to say.

Andy used to bat tennis balls off the back of the church, a rambling old house that was abandoned then. But, last year, a young evangelist had bought the place, knocked down some walls, laid new carpet, and built a stage, all in the precious name of Jesus.

The only heat came from a sheet metal stove the reverend himself had welded. He crammed it with oak until the lid glowed red and the pipe to the old chimney hissed. Men wearing shirts with mother-of-pearl buttons and string ties stood near the stove. They held worn paperback hymnals, the gift of some more prosperous congregation.

The reverend stuck out a hand. "Brother Andy? I'm Jimmy Bolivar. Sister Mavis says you were in Vietnam."

"Yessir." Bolivar had long black hair he kept sweeping back from his forehead, and his compelling black eyes reminded Andy of a lieutenant he'd known, his platoon leader, a West Pointer who'd come and gone without a scratch. Andy felt as though Mavis had set him up, but still he liked

Bolivar. He lowered his head. "I don't hardly know what to do with myself, Reverend."

"Why, serve the Lord, Brother Andy!"

"Amen," Mavis whispered, and clutched Andy's forearm.

A rancher known as Brother Jones stood with his back to the stove and led in "Farther Along" and "The Garden." Bolivar, his breath steaming in the air, stalked the old house, clapping his hands and shouting, "Hallelujah! Praise the Lord!"

"I'd just like to apologize," said Brother Jones. "I got a cold and I cain't hardly sing tonight." He was a dark, baldheaded man whom Andy remembered from his mother's church. Sometimes, in those days, Brother Jones played the saw. But tonight, as the reverend stepped forward to speak, Jones retired to a folding chair by the piano, drew a handsome, flat-top guitar from its case, and strummed as if randomly, punctuating Daws' words.

"We are honored," said Bolivar, "to have a soldier boy with us tonight, Sergeant Andrew Bright. We pray for all the soldier boys everywhere in the world. We are soldiers of the cross!"

"Amen!"

"Will you read along with me in Timothy 3: 2? 'Thou therefore endure hardness, as a good soldier of Jesus Christ. No man that warreth entangleth himself with the affairs of this life; that he may please him who hath chosen him to be a soldier.' Brother, good sister, where the soldiers of nations risk their lives, the soldiers of Christ are *offered* life. Life eternal! Oh, ain't life a great battleground, and Satan our enemy? In my own life—well, I was working, not so long ago, for a printer in Los Angeles. Let me tell you the story.

"I had everything. I had a fine automobile. I had a beautiful boat. There was a beautiful, worldly woman I loved. But I had a hard heart. I had been raised the right way but I denied God. I worshipped *things*."

Every sermon went the same way, Andy thought, even in the army. In the Nam, the born-again soldiers hadn't fared any better than the unregenerates. That is, loving Jesus didn't prevent your getting shot to pieces. Maybe the Bible-thumpers came home less disoriented. Maybe their wives stuck by them more of the time. Maybe.

Brother Jones fell into a soft strumming of "Softly and Tenderly," and a slender, black-haired girl slipped forward to join him at the piano Her voice was so tender and innocent it could break any sinner's heart. Brother Jones closed his eyes and the congregation hushed as if to receive a tongue, because Jones had the gift, but he just did sweet backgrounds for the sweet girl.

"Hallelujah," said Reverend Daws. "Won't you come forward, young man, young woman? Jesus said, 'My peace I give unto you; not as the world giveth. Oh, let not your heart be troubled, neither let it be afraid.' Won't you come?"

"Andy," murmured Mavis. She was crying. "I know how hard it's been for you."

He took her hand. "Yes."

"If you would give your life to God, if you would say to Jesus—"

Andy lifted her hands and kissed them. Then he rose, cried, "Dear Lord!" and slipped forward to the little pine altar. A murmur of approval ran through the congregation, and Brother Jones launched into "Are You Washed in the Blood of the Lamb?" with a rousing up tempo. Andy stared at the girl, whose eyes brimmed with her love for Jesus.

Reverend Jimmy Bolivar placed his hand on Andy's head and said, "Are you lost, soldier boy?"

"I am," said Andy, and closed his eyes, and prayed. I should have prayed in Vietnam, he thought. "Thank you, Jesus!" he shouted. He felt the waves of heat from the stove. He felt Mavis next to him, kneeling, praying, also.

"Jesus, Jesus, how I love you!"

At last he stood, and Brother Jones came up with a word about what a good woman Andy's mother had been, and Andy strapped on his guitar. Bolivar shook Andy's hand and invited him to talk about Vietnam to the young people's group on Sunday. Mavis, her eyes bright and triumphant, stood a distance away, holding their coats.

They hurried into the dark, slipping in the

snow, giggling under the big moon. They climbed into the Chevy and she said she'd make some hot chocolate when they got home. He leaned across and kissed her. She disappeared in the shadow and said, simply, "Andy."

"I'm sorry, Mavis. I *feel* good."

"You're saved, Andy. That's why you feel good."

She stepped out and he ran the Chevy around to the back yard. He came down the hall and stood watching her in the darkness, as she put out milk and sugar and chocolate, and then he stepped into the light. She turned, pushed him back, but he kissed her, anyhow. He ran his hands under her blouse and held her near. He lifted up her skirt and put his hand between her legs.

He picked her up and carried her to his bed and pulled down her underwear and fucked her. Then they undressed and kissed each other all over, and he kept coming into her until she climaxed, and lay moaning, and then lay quietly. He rolled onto his back and stared through the window as he had when he was a child, through the high branches of the cottonwood at the big, cold moon.

After years of trying to succeed with second hand rigs, filling in his time with construction work, George Bright had landed a job with a trucking company that ran out of Liberal, Kansas. He made good money although he hated being on the road so much. Sometimes, he had to deliver to New York. "They only let you in real early in the morning," he said. "I'm outta there 'fore the sun's up, and that suits me. I hate that stinkin' town."

Andy coughed. "It says in the Bible you have to endure hardness."

"Yeah! That's right!" George paused. "Mavis said you came to Jesus. It's the most wondrous feeling! Hadn't been for Mavis—you know how it is. So lonely. And you in the army."

Andy nodded. Somehow, they'd made it through the day. Complaining of a headache, Mavis slipped away after supper, and the old man and Andy sat in the living room, the television turned low to a bowl game.

"She's an awful nice woman," George ventured.

"That's a fact."

"I was worried about being older, but after a while it didn't seem to matter. She loves me for what I am. And, sort of like you, she talked me into going to church again. When your mother passed on—"

Andy sighed. "Can we not talk about my mother? Please?"

George cleared his throat. "I said, 'Mavis, I got this house. It's not so fine, I wouldn't pretend it is, but it's paid for.' And I'll fix it up, I told her. I put in that washer and dryer, and then she wanted a dishwasher. I tell you, Andy, a man goes to a lot of trouble for a woman.

"Of course, she ought to have a dishwasher if she wants one, but women don't understand. You'll find out, one of these days. I had to put in a bigger water heater, and run all new copper in there under the sink, on account of the black pipe was so full of crud. That ain't all. You got to keep your temperature hotter even though you only use your dishwasher every couple days. Here I am on the road two weeks, sometimes, and it runs the bill up for nothin'. That's what a man does for love, I reckon."

"You never even wrote me," Andy said.

"Aw, I meant to, Andrew."

"Nobody wrote me. Not even a fuckin' Christmas card."

"You watch your language in this house. Mavis won't stand for it, I'll tell you that."

Andy walked to the window. "I'm sorry," he said, peering through the curtains.

"You don't want me to talk about your mother, but she was my wife and she was precious to me. I know you don't believe it, but I took her death awful hard. You're welcome here, Andy. You get out of the service and wanta stay here a while, that's fine. I *want* you to. But there you was, almost grown. I didn't know what to do."

"You're just livin' with her, aren't you? You ain't gonna bother to get married."

"That's not true. I think it's been a long day. Everybody's tired. I think you're full of trouble because of the bad experiences you've had. Take an achin' heart to the Lord, I say. And, you know, we'll be prayin' for you."

"You got her bought and paid for with your goddam dishwasher. You just want something to *fuck*."

"Son—"

Andy staggered into the kitchen. The light was strange in this place. He thought he might black out. He stepped into the hall for his coat and, turning, saw Mavis by the bathroom door. She took a drag from her cigarette, blew smoke. She stared as though she didn't know him.

His father had come from the living room. "You sit right down here, Mister. This is my house. Who you think you are?"

"Nobody," he said, pivoting on heel. He marched through the door.

"My name is Andy Bright and I'm just back from the Republic of Vietnam." Phone booths were the coldest places on earth, he thought. There was a long silence, and he wrote her name in the frost.

"I'm sorry," Lindsey said at last.

"You're sorry?"

"I'm sorry you were in Vietnam."

"I was wondrin' if we could maybe get together sometime. I'm home on leave right now and I'm goin' crazy."

"You're goin' crazy, Andy?"

"I never did get along with my daddy and he's livin' with this real religious woman. It's like I got no home."

"I'm *extremely* religious, Andy."

"Oh."

"Just kidding! Listen, there's somebody here right now. If you wanted to do somethin' tomorrow night—"

"Yeah! There used to be this catfish place up in Liberal."

"The Cottonwoods? They have live music!"

"Maybe I could come by around six."

He reeled out of the booth and walked around the Chevy several times. He sat with the door open, smoking cigarettes. I'm all right, he thought. Lindsey thinks so. Just like that, she'd give him a chance! He'd been so gloomy and unsure of himself, skulking around Alva, no wonder things had been tough.

You had to endure hardship to get to heaven. The Bible said so.

He'd see her for a couple of weeks and then she could visit him in Colorado. They could go to Leadville and Aspen and sleep in motels.

He drove out to the Skelly truckstop again and played the pinball machines. He went into the gift shop, where he bought a Stetson and a nice shirt for when Lindsey and he went to Liberal.

"Andy?"

She was blonde, with long, straight hair. What was her name?

"I read in the paper you were back. You're the only boy in our class who had to go over there. I felt so bad for you."

Susan! "What you doing here?"

"I work here, but I need a ride home, Andy. I mean, my mom was—"

"Sure." Why hadn't he thought of Susan before? Well, because he'd never felt much of anything for her. She was just a scrawny little thing from the church, a long way from becoming a woman, in his estimation. She helped him through English their senior year. They shared a study hall, and, occasionally, ate lunch together at the cafeteria.

She'd changed. They got in the Chevy, and she smiled and crossed her legs. And he couldn't remember her eyes flashing like that, or even that she'd ever worn lipstick. "Wanta go somewhere?"

"I've got a seven-thirty."

"A seven-thirty what? Is that a car?"

"That's a class. I go to college. And now you can, too. You're very *bright,* Andy Bright."

He didn't like her pun much, but he laughed. He pulled in front of her house and flipped off the lights. "Let's drive up to Liberal."

"Call me." She reached for the door. "Thanks for the ride."

He leaned across and kissed her.

"You didn't used to be so aggressive."

"I thought about you the whole time I was in 'Nam. I went out there tonight looking for you."

"Liar."

"Why didn't you ever write me?"

"I wrote you three times. You never answered."

He kissed her again and put a hand on her thigh.

"Stop!"

He kissed her hard. She slapped him. "I don't *know* you," she said.

"I wanta fuck you."

She got out of the car. "You were so shy. I'd have gone out with you any time if you'd just *asked* me. Good luck, Andy."

He watched her walk away. He drove downtown for beer, then parked behind his father's rig, thinking of Susan. She was a tease, that was all. He put a hand inside his fly and stroked himself several times.

The thing to do was drop by the truckstop tomorrow and apologize. And send her flowers. They were all suckers for flowers.

Wait a minute. He couldn't get away with screwing two women in the same little town.

Yes, he could. If he timed it right he'd be on the road to Colorado before either of them caught on.

He staggered to the porch and fumbled for his key. You'd think they'd leave the light on. He turned the lock but the door didn't give. He was about to shout for help when he saw his duffel bag and shirts from high school piled on the porch.

"Hey, it's me! Daddy? Mavis!"

He heard Mavis crying.

"Hey, let me in! I belong here!"

A light came on. Through the curtains, he could see shapes moving about in the kitchen.

"Bitch!" he heard the old man say, and Mavis cried and cried.

The light went out.

"Hey, what you doing?" Andy said, and kicked the door. "Well, fuck you!" he yelled, and went down the walk again, carrying the duffel bag and shirts. He stood by his car and shook his fist. "Fuck you, fuck you!"

The pavement was clear and in two hundred miles he met only one car. He topped eighty along the flat stretches and almost went off the road. "I'm drunk," he announced, and got out of the car to urinate. He walked across the flat land among the thistles and yuccas until his headlights were nothing but specks. He sobbed uncontrollably.

"Don't cry," he told himself. "You are a combat veteran. The Bible says to endure hardness!"

He found a Top Forty station broadcasting from Dalhart, Texas, and soon they played some Creedence, but he would have traded the radio for a better heater. He reached Guymon and bought three blankets at a truck stop. He ate cheese crackers and Vienna sausages and drank orange juice, and then he wasn't drunk, but sleepy.

He had a fine car. That was something.

He'd missed a turn somewhere. He was still headed west, but was afraid the road would dead end on one of those huge ranches in New Mexico. He pulled the blankets over him and slept awhile, then woke, deeply chilled.

It was nearly dawn. The sun burst out behind

him over a hulk of dark rock. Andy knew where he was; every school kid knew. Black Mesa. Highest point in Oklahoma.

He even knew the turnoff for the park where his father had taken him once. You followed a gravel road through a ranch, and then paralleled a stream that fell into the canyon. He dragged up fragments of wood and sagebrush, and built a fire. All he had were the Vienna sausages, so he toasted them and toasted his bread, and wolfed everything down with the last of his beer. He grew warm and drowsy by his fire. He liked being so solitary, here on the New Mexico line.

"Beer for breakfast," he said, crawling under his blankets again. "Old Army tradition."

Hallelujah
by and by

DEPUTY JERRY SHOWALTER was off-duty, so he called Nancy Cooley, the waitress at the Midnighter, because he happened to know she was off. He just wanted to get drunk, and screw, but he might throw in a trip to Conway, and dinner at that steakhouse where they had a pretty good country band. On the other hand, it was a Friday, and a storm was coming in; they could just hole up. There was some local weed the sheriff and he confiscated last year: harsh stuff, but surprisingly—deceptively—powerful.

No way she could refuse, but she did. Headache, she claimed. Need to wash your hair, too?

To hell with her. All she ever talked about was her worthless ex-. He hung up.

He opened the refrigerator door, but nothing inspired him. He absolutely wasn't going to cook. Order a pizza? He left the door ajar and went in to turn on the TV. As the picture fluttered into view his mind fluttered also, with an image of olives; he returned to the refrigerator, where he found olives, cheese, and another Miller. He headed for the living room again but caught himself in the mirror: shirtless, wearing his gray Stetson and the red cut-offs he'd had since high school. The bullet would, healed in a bead as if welded, shone dully across one bicep: *handsome*. Women loved it. God bless the North Vietnamese.

He set the beer and food on the dining table and said, "Awright. Up against the wall." He doubled with laughter but then stopped, stepped near the TV, frowned.

There was a coven of witches. Each was dressed in a flowing white gown, clinging and transparent. They danced in a circle, while on a dais their mistress, her long legs flashing amid wisps of smoke, made incantations. Wonderful. Hard to believe it—wicked satellite television— could ever have arrived in godly little Holbrook.

Cut to a lonely mountain road, a man with car trouble, thunder and lightning. The man was a priest: good and evil were coming up. The priest looked worriedly up the hill, toward the witches' decayed mansion.

Jerry drew a match to a wad of local stuff in a pipe, coughed, and chugged half a Miller. The phone rang, and he leaped to his feet, while another self seemed to float up, and slowly settle in. He struggled, in the mirror, for a serious arrangement of his face.

"How you, tonight?"

"Sheriff. I'm . . . all by my . . . lonesome." Jerry felt foolish saying "by" and then saying "my." He stifled an urge to giggle, and to invite the sheriff into his Friday night world of witches and weed.

"Tornado watch. You hear?"

"Yeah . . . "

"Your night off. Jerry, you know I'd go myself, but somethin' about supper, I cain't pinpoint it, but sick as a dog there a while. Well. George and Colleen Lambert's little boy. Crippled?"

"Right." It seemed that the priest had only been masquerading as a priest. He was really a thief on the run. He'd slipped into the darkness after the head witch, and now they stood naked in a clearing in the woods, in the electric moonlight.

"Strange story. Colleen took the boy to revival meetin', out on the old Avery place, and this Leroy Parsons healed him. Or claimed to. The boy walked around normal for two days, only he died, Jare, early this afternoon."

Jerry stood erect, his duty shaping. "That's an awful thing, Paul."

"I got a call—George is gone. He was sittin' down at the Midnighter, gettin' drunk and talkin' crazy, like how he was gonna kill this preacher. Several men with him, eggin' him on. And I know Colleen's out there, to the meetin', right now. I'm just afraid—"

Jerry reached awkwardly for his shirt. "Weapons?" he asked, using the army word, the serious word, rather than "guns."

The sheriff seemed surprised. "Well, maybe. Maybe they'll go on home, and sleep it off. I want you to drive on out there, anyways. Take it easy. I might swing by later myself."

Jerry hunched the phone under his chin as he reached for the Glock. "Arrest this Perkins?"

"I . . . don't know. Could you call it man-slaughter? I don't know; you talk to him. After the service—don't break up no meetin'. You okay, Jare? You do this?"

"Sure, Paul."

"You call in my house. 10-4?"

"10-4." Now he drew on the city's trousers and his army raincoat, and stood before the TV to finish strapping on the Glock 22. The false priest, drunk on witches' brew, lay stripped on the dais. The witches danced ever faster while their mistress chanted something scary. A knife gleamed in the moonlight. Great stuff, Jerry thought. Right here in Holbrook.

Jerry pointed the city's big Plymouth toward the road for a quick getaway. Maybe there was never a time, stoned or sober, when visions of chasing down fugitives, his Glock aimed out the window, wasn't a little on his mind. Jerry stepped from the Plymouth—and was in Nam.

Floating down the hill, the good news came to greet him:

> *I'll*
> *fly away oh glo-ry*
> *I'll*
> *fly away*

When I die
Hallelujah by and by
I'll
Fly away

He hadn't heard the song since he was a boy.
The old guilt rose inside him, the urge to cry—he
shook it away. He'd been raised a Freewill Baptist
which filled his mind with spooks, but still, in high
school, he packed Millers in a cooler and man-
euvered other Baptists, female, into the wide back
seats of his powerful cars. *Entirely of their own free*
will.

And yet later, full of guilt, he sought out redemption, and adopted a piety just as fierce as his
sins. He'd stand before the congregation, chording
a guitar and singing, in a passable baritone, "I Got
a Mansion." Yes, the church always pulled him
back from destruction. Then there was Vietnam, a
lot of dead men and a lot of dope—and no more
redemption.

Just aging knees, and a cigarette cough.

Lightning lit the way, but the darkness was
otherwise nearly complete. He was more stoned
than he'd realized, and it seemed to take hours to
climb the hill. The stuff crept up on you like real
dope, like that opium he'd smoked another black
night.

He'd staggered from the bunker to take a piss
and seemingly *flown* across to the mess hall, where
he stole some bananas, and fell asleep. He
dreamed he cruised the Holbrook Main Street

with a gigantic rabbit. He fucked the rabbit, or tried to, until he woke to a shower of beautiful lights. Beautiful . . . *mortars,* he slowly realized. He sat there watching them come in, and explode left and right. The opium pinned him down. He could cheerfully have watched as his arm came off.

He was fifty feet from the revival tent now, at the point where light gave way to shadow. Heat rolled from beneath the canvas—the lights, the sweating bodies packed tightly. The air itself was still, warm, almost wet, as the storm hovered. The light beckoned, and he turned into it helplessly— but then was repelled.

His head cleared. He'd felt the same, slightly hostile wave he used to feel when he brought to church a girl not bearing the stamp of approval.

"I'm the Law," he murmured, gathering himself. And the Law was sufficient.

Yet even as his duty rose in him, he thought of the witches in their diaphanous gowns, and reached out involuntarily, grasping the damp air.

One hundred feet away, down the sawdust aisle, Leroy Perkins bent left and right in his pulpit, shaking it as he spoke. His white shirt so clung to his skin that the lines of hair and gaunt muscle shone through; sweat ran down his bare scalp to bristle in the creases of his face. His thin nose dropped and jerked back sharply, like a beak. He was so tall that he himself seemed to be framed in the picture of the Redeemer that hung behind, and there was such energy in his eyes even Jerry was affected. He might have rushed forward, a boy again, in tearful submission.

The Law, he thought, the *Law*. He trod the edge of darkness around to the side.

"Praise the Lord!" the crowd chorused. Jerry drew parallel to the altar, draped with white muslin to cover the communion. No, not communion, not at a revival. What? He saw Colleen Lambert—not the skinny, poultry plant worker who'd have turned no one's eye, but a delicate, somehow younger-looking woman in a white gown. She stood by the altar, staring up at Parsons and then, with a marvelous radiance, over the crowd. Her lips moved: "Yes, Jesus. Yes, Jesus."

Jerry reeled backward. He'd been clapping his hands, and singing along with Colleen as she led the crowd. He tore his eyes downhill. There was no sign of a drunken Lambert, and he figured this was a wild goose chase. Lambert and his buddies were drowning their sorrows elsewhere, out of the storm, perhaps even in the company of witches.

He turned in panic. He should have reported to the sheriff by now. Still, he paused; Perkins had paused.

A light rain fell. The crowd rocked steadily to the beat of the generator, their faces flushed, molten. Colleen's high, sugary voice broke off its song. There was a hush, and Jerry knew a tongue would still the air.

A fat man jerked to his feet; every eye fled to him in an instinctive, electric movement. Heat and light seemed to flow through him, outward to his flabby arms, stretching shakily toward Heaven. "Kohala ma shigima khi . . . " he said, or chanted, building on the "khi," stretching it out in anguish, even pain. "Sheela magunda. Sheela magunda. Kohala ma shigima khi-ee—"

His wife, fat as he, bent in a faint, her face given over to seizure. Her small son, looking up with serious blue eyes, attempted to prop her up. His palms sank into her stomach, and she teetered like a piece of furniture. Her husband wept on obliviously, in bursts, in gasps, lapsing finally into a quivering speechlessness. The crowd, moaning with the rising hiss of rain, floated on high emotion, then fell away with the fat man into silence as he came to himself with the final, repeated syllables: " . . . Machi."

Jerry, too, was transported, staring into so many eyes, red from crying—or deep blue, following tears. Parsons' interpretation seemed like a scolding from Jerry's childhood: "Behold! I am He that liveth, and was dead. So ye also that believeth upon me shall be snatched away in the twinkling of an eye, and have eternal life."

"Amen," sobbed the crowd.

"The beast shall rise, and causeth all to suffer plagues and abominations, until they cry out for the mountains to fall upon them. Behold! I come as a thief in the night, I come quickly, and my reward is with me. I am the alpha and the omega, amen."

"Amen!"

A silence, a sort of peace, settled. Jerry fell back into the corn and turned downhill. Suddenly, the army raincoat and Glock 22 weren't enough; he reached for his pipe and a pinch of weed. The rain fell steadily, but he managed a light as he crouched by a van. His lungs filled with harshness, and then he came loose from himself, and seemed to hover above the corn and swollen river. A huge dog jumped against the van's rear window, pressed its snout against the glass, and snarled. Jerry leaped away.

He reached the Plymouth, where he sat, unable to think. The rain fell heavily now, and he couldn't see. The car was an island, with water tearing around it, down the corn rows. He took a cigarette from the dash and smoked it halfway down, probed for himself, found nothing. In little notches of feeling, like a spring unwinding to a flat strip of steel, he found the middle again. Someone called to him. "Okay, Paul," he said.

"Where you been?"

"Okay."

"Lambert show?"

"Nobody here . . . but the faithful." A white scallop arced across the black horizon, and the corn seemed like rows of silvery thin men, whipping about in the wind.

"Probly went home to sleep it off."

"Roger that."

"Roger! Well. Rainin' there?"

"Comin' down. Pretty good." A diagram for his words appeared in the air, like a wiring schematic. Shape up, soldier!

"I should come out. You think? You sound . . . look, I understand, Friday night and all, caught you by surprise. Rainy night. All settled in."

"Fine." Jerry felt that he was fine. "Wish that damn service was—" He caught the outline of his face in the rearview mirror. The cigarette made him glow. His eyes were his dead father's eyes, he realized, and turned in the seat, as though the old man were behind him. He swallowed a sob. "O-ver," he remembered to say, and giggled, because of the long pause.

"Right. Over, Jerry. I'm on my way. How copy?"

"Solid copy, Paul, roger dodger. Let's call in some Redleg. Outie out."

Redleg? Sheets of black cut the black; beneath lightning, the stalks in the long rows had become soldiers marching uphill, rifles at high port. Combat mission! He laughed, but was serious. Redleg? He could almost hear the artillery whistling in. He slid out of the car and immediately bogged down between corn rows, the water flowing into his shoes, around the sprung, wiry roots. He jerked up his head like a hound. Cold air shot through his lungs, and he felt tall. There!

On the road above, out from the hilltop, head-lights appeared, and a car stopped. Lambert, he thought. He'd expected them to pull in at the bottom of the hill, with all the other cars. He needed to hurry.

The headlights winked out softly in the rain. Jerry imagined an engine shutting off, and footsteps on the sodden grass. There was a fence, and a little woods by the road. He could be there before them. He fingered the Glock's safety; it was the lever switching to "Auto" on an M-16. He extended his arms low, one hand on the barrel guard, one finger poised by the trigger.

The corn sawed across his chest, tugged him back; but now light from the tent thrust into the rain, and Jerry could see the prophet standing by the shrouded altar. Looking out of the rain, Parsons appeared to Jerry as if through glass, like one of those paperweights in which life is suspended and inaccessible. The prophet raised his hands, and cried out, "God raise this boy!"

The boy? His imaginary rifle stock in the mud, one boot bent to grip the grass of the hilltop, Jerry prepared to rush. A cough rose from the woods, even as Parsons spoke again: "Believe! Believe upon Him, and rise, rise!"

Out of the woods came two old men, and George Lambert. Lambert was a big man, balding, with a creased face and beak-like nose not unlike the prophet's. They might have been brothers.

His eyes were bright when, in the rain, they should not have shone at all. Oh, the weed! And now Lambert moved too quickly to be comprehended, and Jerry was paralyzed. Energy from the tent—and dread the sheriff was on his way—pushed Jerry forward.

"Hold it," he managed. "Hold it right there." He felt his tone projected boldness, but also neutrality. "It's the Law."

The men halted, but the determination in their motion seemed to swing on ahead. Lambert had an M-1, Jerry saw, and the two old men carried shotguns. Lambert nodded fiercely, shaking rain from his hat. "The Law is shit," he said.

"Drop—those—weapons."

The old men complied, but Lambert marched on for the tent. Jerry ran after, or the soldier in him did; he broke suddenly into the bright lights, and was dazzled. Then he lifted up his feet and floated, until at last he tackled Lambert at the very end of the center aisle. Lambert heaved to his feet but Jerry clung like a bobcat, and the two of them staggered down a row of empty folding chairs until they collapsed in the sawdust.

Jerry knew Lambert was stronger, but he was possessed of a miraculous strength—the strength of the Law, he thought. His righteous fists pummeled Lambert until the man's face was cut, and puckered. Jerry slowly rose, studying the blood on his knuckles. Had he done well? Had he served the Law?

No one looked his way. It was as though there had been no fight, and yet how the people sang!

The rain made a wall behind them. The two

old men peered out of it, and receded. panting, like coyotes at the edge of fire.

"Fool," croaked Lambert, raising an arm. *"Look."*

His wife, Colleen, pulled away the muslin of the altar, revealing her dead son. Parsons raised his hands to still the crowd, while Colleen gazed up wearily, but with beautifully clear eyes. Parsons, standing straight and tall as a rocket, placed a palm on the boy's forehead. "Raise him! Raise this boy, oh Lord!"

"Kill him!" Lambert screamed. "Kill him!"

The boy rose. While his body remained on the altar, another dwelled in the air, rose high and descended to the floor, then walked shakily to his mother. Even as she embraced him the boy slid away and flew up high as a tower, a white plume just grazing the canvas roof.

Jerry believed. He believed that he, too, might rise. He had no strength to resist as Lambert took the Glock from his hands, and aimed it at Parsons. Two quick shots, and the prophet slumped forward, a mushrooming red coloring his white chest. Wrong, thought Jerry. *Wrong.*

Yet Parsons rose, and held out his hands to Colleen—shot down even as she fled to him. She rose. The prophet took her in his arms, and they rose through the roof with the boy.

Lambert staggered by the altar, firing through the hole in the roof. When the hammer clicked on an empty chamber, he sat, head between his knees.

Jerry gasped. He walked down the aisle, looking up through the torn canvas. Rain drilled at him. Wind tumbled around him in broken shrieks. He held out a hand to Lambert for the Glock, and Lambert jumped up, a deep violence, maybe evil itself, in his eyes. He swung the weapon against Jerry's face, cutting his forehead. Then he ran.

The generator skipped a beat. The lights flickered, and came on again. Jerry lifted his bleeding face, and before him, bodies escaped their bodies, and flew away. He covered his ears to shut out the shrieks. The generator stopped, and the lights went out.

He would have run, but his legs had no strength. He fell, and crawled. A pole came crashing down. Jerry's hands reached out in the darkness, and grasped mud. Rough canvas settled over him, and he couldn't breathe.

Behind Enemy Lines

"OH," KILLER MURMURED, and clutched at his jaw, because his teeth hurt. The pain had awakened him. He'd had a bad dream, too, but couldn't remember what about. He'd had many bad dreams lately. His teeth hurt him in his sleep and caused his mind to conjure horrible things.

He dropped his feet to the floor. He knew where he was: in the bus, on the island, in the river. "Wolf!" he called, and from beneath the metal floor he heard a growl.

Killer stepped outside, naked except for his shoes and ragged shorts. He reached into his mouth with a thumb and forefinger and pressed on a molar. Eat something, get busy, and he'd forget his pain.

He filled the coffee pot, then dropped potatoes and onions in a kettle. He hung both pot and kettle over his cooking pit, and built a fire. He headed for the river, carrying his .22 rifle, swatting at mosquitoes. Bullfrogs croaked out a full chorus—their farewell until another nightfall.

Wolf crept from behind and gently caught Killer's shin with his teeth. "Think maybe I'll make some wolf stew," Killer said, and the animal whimpered, and rolled in the grass, before slipping into the brush.

Killer reached the gravel bar at the head of the island. Rain had to be falling upcountry because the water was high. Ordinarily in summer he could have walked five hundred feet farther, casting lines, without getting his feet wet.

He plunged off the submerged bar and wriggled down in the muddy water to his fish trap, but he had no fish today. He broke the surface and swam a few strokes, drifting with the curls of fog that still caressed the water. A red-tailed hawk sailed low, gliding just above the surface before powering upward again to cruise at treetop above the swamp. Killer dropped his feet to the slimy bottom, fearful of leeches. They lived in water like this. He eased forward, goop squeezing between his toes, until he found gravel.

Wolf lay in a first patch of sun. He'd sniffed out a nest of young cottontails and, when they panicked, tracked them each down their little tunnels under the matted grass. He trapped one, snapped its back in his teeth, and sucked the steaming meat from its skin. Now he opened his eyes, and growled low.

Not fifty feet away, across the channel on the Missouri side, the doe's ears flicked from out of the brown and green oak leaves. She darted her head about, nudged the open air as if it were palpable, and then quickly, delicately stepped to the water.

Killer sat on a rickety dinette chair he'd brought back from the Platte County Landfill. He pulled on his socks. He heard Wolf growling and then saw the doe drinking. He shot her through the eye.

It took him half the morning to butcher the doe, but the work kept him so busy he didn't think about how much his teeth hurt. He threw the entrails to the fish and cut out the haunches and all the lean meat and threw the remainder into the brush for the coons. Blood soaked into the muddy bank but the river still rose. In a few days the blood and stench would be washed clean, and deer would come again.

He loaded the meat into his canoe and paddled around the head of the island. A barge carrying scrap iron chugged upstream, and on the Kansas side a farmer walked along the top of the dike, looking out. The farmer waved at a man on the barge but neither of them noticed Killer, who guided the canoe in among a stand of sycamores and began carrying the venison to his camp.

Killer knew there were such things as licenses and hunting seasons but the state couldn't catch you unless you went to a processing station, and they couldn't catch you, either, if they didn't know you were alive. Barge workers and fishermen saw him occasionally, but there wasn't much to see. He had thin hair and a matted beard and he was brown like the river. The island looked like more of the swamp, rather than an island, and you wouldn't have thought anyone could live on it, or want to. Even in the winter the high ground where Killer's bus sat was hard to see.

Every time he killed a deer he had trouble with Wolf, who tried to rip open the abdomen for the liver, or threw dirt on the carcass, or even urinated on the meat after he'd gorged himself. So Killer coaxed the animal into the pen he'd made out of chain-link that had come drifting downriver atop a broken shed. Wolf growled and clawed at the fence as Killer brought up the pieces of deer. "Shut up," Killer said, and the animal stared at him with his yellow eyes. Killer threw him a foreleg.

He salted the rest of the meat and strung it on greasy wires inside a metal feed hopper. Then he connected some thirty feet of pipe back to his stove. He shoveled up coals, covered them with chunks of hickory, and closed the damper. He'd keep a low fire for several days.

He opened the pen and Wolf walked out with an aggrieved air. Killer stood astride of him and kneaded his ribs and the animal caught Killer's wrist in his mouth, then rolled over and lay near the cooking pit.

Wolf was truly a wolf, orphaned from a pack that had wandered down the river bottom all the way from the Dakotas. They'd ranged in the swamp for nearly a year, preying on highland sheep and poultry, until farmers shot them. Killer found Wolf, clumsy and not yet weaned, floundering by the water. He scared the pup; it ran into the water and nearly drowned.

As for whether Killer was truly a killer, he himself couldn't have said. He was christened when he bought his .22 at a garage sale in Platte City. "This gun shoot straight?" he asked. "I want to kill deer with it. They get in my garden."

"Shoot a deer with a .22?" the woman asked. "What a killer!"

He liked what the woman said, and afterwards thought of himself as Killer, though if you had asked him directly he would have told you his name was Robert Coogan.

"Hush."

He sat up. All was black. "What?"

"They're coming."

They lay inside a thicket of bamboo, waiting for the major. Tiny boats drifted by, their lanterns flickering, on a river so broad you couldn't see across it. In the dark he couldn't tell the difference between land and water, because both places were wet. It had rained for as long as he could remember.

"Take the Claymore."

The man thrust the little generator into Killer's hand and rolled over to prop himself behind the machine gun. Killer's eyes stung from the rain and he didn't know which way to look. It was always raining and it was always dark.

"Now. You hear?"

He brought the halves of the generator together and an arc of light lit up the river and six men on the trail. Behind them, around them, the eyes of animals stared, before the eerie light went out and a soldier screamed and a fish plopped on Killer's head. Killer screamed, too, as the man beside him opened up with the machine gun, firing at the image of men still imprinted on the air, on his and Killer's eyes, and then at the blackness.

"Lincoln," Killer murmured, remembering his companion's name for the first time in a long while, though he'd had the dream before. More a memory than a dream, perhaps, and he lay without moving in the dark, panting a little, trying to figure things out. The rain pounded against the bus. It was that darkest time of the morning when the birds and insects don't sing and no dog howls.

His teeth ached fiercely and he stumbled about with his flashlight, searching for aspirin. He turned on the radio just to hear a voice, but the batteries were dead. He could tell by the silence in the woods that it was not quite five o'clock.

"Jesus!" he shouted, as the pain shot through his eyes.

He staggered outside. Pools of water stood around the cooking pit, and rain fell steadily. He sat beside the sputtering coals, holding his jaw. For years there had been a dull pain, but now a wild animal was inside his mouth. He clinched his teeth and beat on his mandible with a fist.

He built up the fire, made coffee, ladled out stew. He stoked the stove again. Yellow eyes glinted in the woods, and Wolf materialized. Killer fed him, saw that he had water, and shut him in the chain-link pen. Otherwise, the animal would follow him into Platte City.

Killer couldn't have a timber wolf at his heels. He caused enough of a stir all by himself.

Halfway to Platte City stood a store where you could buy bait and beer and snack food. Killer rose from the swamp and came around the corner abruptly, almost stumbling over two young women sitting with sodas. They weren't local. They had fancy bicycles and wore tight, short pants and odd-looking helmets. "Ex*cuse* me," said one, drawing up her legs, and then she just stared.

"God," murmured the other, as Killer went in the door. "Are we in the sticks, or what?"

The man behind the counter grunted hello. He'd tried to strike up a conversation once or twice but Killer didn't understand him very well. Killer couldn't think of anything to say, but liked the man because he never tried to run him off.

Killer bought aspirin and a can of peaches. Plastic spoons were free and he took six. He went out to the picnic table and sat washing down aspirin with peach nectar. The peaches stung his teeth but he didn't have to chew them. He also liked the peaches in green cans. Apricots were even better but there weren't as many in a case.

The women didn't look at Killer now. They put on their backpacks and strange helmets and peddled away in the drizzle. They were from Mars.

He walked along the Interstate, then crossed a fence and began thinning Jordan Prescott's apples. Killer liked the work because it went on hard and monotonously for a month or so, and then was done. He liked that Jordan was a bachelor and didn't talk much. In October Killer returned to pick the apples and Jordan always gave him two bushels of Jonathans besides paying in cash. Killer hated checks because without a driver's license no one would cash them.

Three years before, in a winter when the channel ran dry and the swamp froze over, Jordan gave Killer the school bus. It ran just enough for Killer to drive it to the island. He'd been living in a lean-to covered over with sheet iron and dirt.

It was all right to thin apples in the rain because you stayed cool. But Killer's teeth started hurting again. Jordan found him sitting at the top of a picking ladder, thumb and index finger pressing hard on the roof of his mouth. "Bobby! Go to a dentist!"

"No money."

"Can't you go to the VA, across the river?"

Killer considered. "Yes," he said. "I know where that is."

"I got business in Saint Joe. Take you to the crossroads. Poor day to work, anyhow."

Killer stared out the pickup as they passed the women on bicycles. He'd known a woman who looked like the one riding in front. That was when he lived in the city. Louise. She lived up above.

"Going cross-country, I spose," Jordan said.

"Yeah."

Jordan pulled over. "Feel bad not taking you all the way."

Killer nodded.

"Got to get some spray for the beetles. It's such a wet year I can't hardly keep up. Don't know *what* kinda crop I'm gonna have." Jordan pulled out his worn billfold. "Can I give you something for a haircut?"

Killer held the money. It was more than he would have made if he'd worked all morning.

Jordan eased out the clutch. "Little trim wouldn't hurt. Beard, too, Bobby."

Killer walked along the highway to Leavenworth through the low ground. The ditches were filled with water and pools stood in the soy beans. The sun came out briefly and he began sweating. The women on bicycles swished by, and Killer dropped his head.

"Hi, how are you?" Louise asked, and Killer

waved and smiled. He liked Louise. He knew he had done something to make her unhappy in the city but it was long ago.

"*Boy*friend," the woman behind her called.

"Jan, the poor thing."

"Romance on the *prair*ie."

Killer had forgotten about women. He didn't dream of them any more. In Platte City they paid no attention to him, but he could tell that the woman on the bicycle meant to be nice. She wasn't really Louise, however. Where had he known Louise?

It began raining again. He stood on the bridge to Leavenworth, watching the water churn. Ten miles to the south was his island, and Wolf. He'd never seen the river so high.

The women were gone forever.

It was Monday and the barbershop was closed. He didn't want to go to a barber, anyhow. He didn't care about the top of his head. It was his teeth that needed fixing.

He walked past the guard station, expecting to be hailed, but no one was on duty. A green truck swished by in the mist and he stepped off the road, climbed a spongy bank and disappeared inside a willow grove, where he surprised a flock of Canadian geese. They hissed at him and he ran into the cemetery, where the rows of white markers marched down to the river. He came to the water. He couldn't see where the river ended, and Missouri began. Great trees floated by, and a dead pig on a raft.

He turned on heel and walked straight for a massive, brick building that must have squatted here through a dozen wars. He found an entrance and sloshed across a marble floor; to his left and right were offices. Ahead, blocking access to a long, dim corridor, stood a big man in whites. A guard, Killer thought. He sought out an old man who pushed a laundry hamper.

"What?" The old man stared at Killer. He wore thick glasses that magnified his eyes.

"I need to get my teeth fixed."

"Oh." The old man pointed across the hall, where several men waited in a row of chairs.

Killer walked along the edge of the marble so that he could see inside the office, where three women worked at computers. He studied them for a long time and stared at himself reflected on a stainless steel post. He combed his hair back with his fingers and tugged at his gray beard. His teeth were black. Did that mean that they would soon fall out, because they were dead? But they weren't dead, or they wouldn't hurt him so.

He charged the office like it was high ground but then stopped abruptly and sat.

"Brother," said the man next to him. "Who you with over there?"

Killer's legs were shaking but he leaped up and went through the door. He stood before the first desk, not knowing what to say.

"Sir?" The woman didn't look up. She had red fingernails that were so long it didn't look like she'd be able to type, but her fingers kept moving.

"I have to get my teeth fixed," Killer managed. He swept back his hair again. A pool formed under his shoes.

"You're a patient here?"

"I live by myself. Wolf and me."

The woman still didn't look up. "Name?"

He told her. She began tapping rapidly, looking up at him once, and blinking, then back at her screen. "Still raining out there?"

"Raining like crazy."

"They're evacuating some of the low areas." She shook her head. "No record of you, sir."

"I just want to get my teeth fixed."

"You may need to contact a private practitioner. At this time the Veterans' Department does not offer outpatient dental care."

Killer stared. "I was with the Cav."

"Sir, you can't just walk in and get your teeth worked on. You will need to go to a civilian facility."

Killer propped a hand on the woman's desk and bent near her, so that she had to look at him. "I don't have any money. Jordon said you have dentists here."

The woman swallowed. Her eyes widened. She scooted her chair to the wall. "The Veterans Department does not offer outpatient dental care at this time. Sir."

< < > >

Killer sat on the steps, watching the rain blow across the great parking lot, and toward the river. It would never stop, he thought. And he had to go out in it, back through the town and across the bridge and downriver ten miles. He would be long after dark arriving. Wolf would be crazy.

"Goddam monsoon out there." Leaning against the wall was a tall, lean man with closely-cropped black hair. He had a brown face stained almost black from his heavy beard. He wore an ear-ring. It was the man who had called him brother.

He offered Killer a cigarette, which Killer took even though he didn't smoke. The man struck a light and they stood blowing smoke into the rain. "John Oglethorpe," the man said.

"They call me Killer."

"Unfucking real, man. I was in the Cav, too. When you there?"

Killer concentrated. "I don't know. I was in the delta, and then I . . . went back."

"You done two tours? No wonder you're so fucked up."

"I—"

"Hey, no sweat. I'm a sick man myself. Why else would I be hanging out at the VA?"

Killer flipped the cigarette away. It gave him a headache. "I just wanted to get my teeth fixed."

"Heard the entire sad story. Here's a man don't have a nickel, coulda got blowed away in the service of his country, they won't even fix his teeth. See, you can't be a patient unless you already *are* one. Heard that before? I mean, it ain't the army but it's damn close. What you need to do, I'm telling you because I *been* there, man, is get drunk. Totally, stinking, dog-rotten, dead drunk. Then you can check into de-tox 'cause you have an alcohol problem, and they'll fix your teeth. You copy, brother?"

Killer shook his head. "I got to get back to Wolf."

"Ah." Oglethorpe laughed. "You're a married man."

They sat drinking in Oglethorpe's camper. They were parked on a knoll in the graveyard looking down on the river. It kept raining and it was so dark Killer thought that the day must be done, but Oglethorpe told him it was only three-thirty. By four Killer's head was spinning. "I'm worried about Wolf," he said, and reached for the door, but then Oglethorpe handed him another plastic cup filled with fire.

"I am a fucked-up individual," Oglethorpe explained. "There is agreement on that point. The question is whether I am one hundred percent fucked up or only maybe forty percent. If I was one hundred percent I could get my own place."

"I live in a bus," Killer announced.

"On an island. With this big dog looks like a wolf."

"*Is* a wolf."

"Can't be no wolf, man. They killed all the wolves. I got to piss."

So did Killer. He staggered across the asphalt and fell down in the grass by a white marker. The river covered the entire world. It wasn't brown any more. It was black.

Oglethorpe urinated on one of the stones. *"Pissing* in the rain," he sang.

"Not right," Killer said.

"It's a fucking major, son. Who cares about a goddam dead major?"

"Officers—" But Killer was confused. An entire house floated by. He should climb onto the house and float down to Wolf. He threw a bottle at a window and fell backward and rain poured into his mouth. He closed his eyes and rolled over in the mud and then he heard gunfire. Oglethorpe was shooting an M-16 at a cat sailing by on a door.

Killer didn't want the cat to die. "Give me that gun!"

"Fuck you, dude!"

Killer tried to grab the rifle but Oglethorpe twisted it away and brought the stock down in Killer's stomach. Killer dropped into a pool and then struggled to his knees. He vomited.

Oglethorpe opened up again on the cat but all his rounds fell short. Killer lay in the water and thought, they're coming for me, I'm dead. Then he rushed Oglethorpe from behind and clubbed him with his clenched hands and tore away the rifle. He sprayed the water, emptying out the magazine, and as he did a green truck drew near, lights on. Two MPs got out and stood in their gray slickers.

"He's crazy!" Oglethorpe screamed. "He's back in Nam!"

"Easy," one of the MPs said. "Throw down your weapon."

Killer dropped the rifle in the mud. He raised his hands high.

"Go for it, brother," Oglethorpe said, and threw a wild swing. Killer stumbled after him, blinded by the rain and the headlights, and an MP cold cocked him.

"Your history," the woman said.

There was a black man in the group, Howard, whom Killer thought he knew from somewhere. There were two white men who grinned, nodded, but never spoke. There was John Oglethorpe, who talked too much. And there was this woman who kept asking questions. "Robert," she said quietly. "Do you want to give us your history today?"

"I don't know much about history," he said.

"She mean your life story," Howard said. "Before you was a hopeless drunk."

"I am not a drunk."

"Just hopeless, then."

"You know about the flood, don't you, Robert?" the woman said. "You know that your dog drowned."

He nodded but didn't believe her. Wolf was smart. Wolf would swim until the water rose to the top of the fence.

"Do you feel that you have a problem with alcohol?" the woman asked.

Killer looked at Oglethorpe. "I do," he said, nodding.

"But you just told Howard that you don't drink."

"He was in denial!" Oglethorpe said.

"John," the woman said. "Let Robert answer for himself."

"In the city," Killer said, and maybe it was true, because he didn't remember. "I'd drink all day and then I'd pass out."

"I see," the woman said, as if she weren't convinced. She glanced at her notes and then at Oglethorpe. "How do your teeth fit, Robert?"

"Good!"

"I understand they're serving corn on the cob tonight." She smiled. "What do you think?"

"I grow corn on the island," Killer said. "Only the deer come after it."

"Shit," Howard said. "Doc made a joke. Where they find this hillbilly dude?"

"Man's a hero, fucker," Oglethorpe said. "Saw some serious shit in Laos."

Howard threw his hands out expansively. "Shittin' me, motherfucker."

"Goddam Silver Star!"

"Okay, okay," the doctor said. "Robert is giving his history. We need to respect each other here. Do you recall getting the medal, Robert?"

He didn't know the name of the village. He didn't know the name of the river. It was raining and he couldn't see and the pilot kept talking crazy talk. The pilot had black splotches on his face, and puckering cuts. He looked like a monster in the movies.

"They beat the man," Oglethorpe said. "But you got there, Bobby. You found him!"

Rifle fire popped out of the trees behind the wharf and the major went down. He couldn't move. His legs quivered and melted together in the mud. You couldn't tell what was legs and what was mud and what was water. "Shoot me!" he screamed. "I'm dead, shoot me!"

Killer crawled in the weeds by the river. He sank in the mud and clawed his way up again frantically, looking for Lincoln. But Lincoln was hit. He fell without a sound. He lay in the water staring at Killer, and the pilot went on blubbering, and the major screamed for Killer to shoot him.

"Jesus H. Christ!" Howard said. "What you do?"

Killer shook his head. "I killed them."

The doctor was alarmed. "The major!"

"I killed *them!*"

"He mean the bad dudes," Howard said. "Ones fucked over the aviator."

Killer pointed angrily at a tall old window. "They were two of them. They came from the village where the pilot was. I saw them."

"You killed them," the doctor said. "You remember."

"*Got* to kill them," Oglethorpe said, shaking his head.

One of the grinning, silent men spoke. *"Got to."*

"And then, Robert?" the woman asked. "You're doing just fine. Then?"

He shut his eyes. "I went out on the dock and—and there was a boat. I went to the pilot because they were all dead. I shook him real hard. He crawled in, and then I got the major. He—he was—"

"In shock," the doctor said. "He was in shock."

"I just dragged him over. He was all covered with—"

"What about the village?" Oglethorpe asked. "Were they coming from the village?"

"I . . . couldn't see. Rain everywhere." Killer shook his head. "I got Lincoln and put him in the bottom except I knew he was dead. There was a little motor on the boat. The pilot, he—"

"How'd you know which way to go?"

"I went . . . *somewhere*. Off in the rain. And they found us."

"The navy?"

"The . . . the Thais."

"The Thais!" Oglethorpe said. "But how?"

"That's fine," the doctor said. She smiled again. "We'll talk more about this at our appointment, that's fine. Good, Robert."

"Good?" Oglethorpe said. "I guess so!"

"Damn good," Howard said.

It was good to eat food with teeth that didn't hurt. It was good to play ping-pong. It was good to go to the PX. It was good to listen to the radio.

It was good to watch a movie. It was good to stare down upon the swollen river from this dry place.

It was good to lie on his bunk and look up at the rain bleeding down the skylight; he watched the rain hour after hour, imagining Wolf swimming in the rising water. He lay with his arms outstretched, perfectly still, but in his mind he moved his hands and swam just as Wolf swam, floating on the flood that slowly rose beneath him, never panicking, conserving his strength until the moment of escape. He seemed to burst through the skylight just as Wolf clambered over the fence.

Maybe Wolf would find his way to the Dakotas. Somewhere there were other wolves. He'd look down on the river from a high, sunny slope, and not even remember where he'd been.

"Disability," Oglethorpe announced. They wouldn't let you smoke in your bunk any more so he always sat on the rear steps by the fire bucket. "No way they'll turn you down. You're a lucky sonuvabitch! One hundred percent!"

"Oh," Killer said, leaning back on his hands and closing his eyes, thinking how odd it was to talk to people, to listen, to reply. "That's good."

"Money for nothing? Hell, yes, that's good." Oglethorpe laughed and flipped his cigarette into the drizzle. "Good as it gets."

\

Rest Stop

OVER THE HOLIDAY weekend, the group was running two soft drink and coffee stands at rest stops north of Tampa. I was headed back to Missouri. This would be last chance to see them.

Our leader—whom we called Wombat after his call sign in Vietnam—had told us that charitable organizations could make as much as $2000 in a single night. "Just put up a sign that says, "Donations accepted."

"And look pitiful?"

"You shouldn't have any trouble there, Irish."

Wombat was a short man with a beard who had a story of parachuting into North Vietnam. They were in a spy plane studded with electronic equipment. Ten kilometers north of the DMZ, they hit a cloud of flak, and both engines caught fire. The captain pushed the destruct button because of all the secrets on board. *There they were* in the impenetrable jungle—but somehow they regrouped, and followed a river toward the DMZ. They were pursued, of course, and the soldiers at the marine firebase nearly wasted them. *The Deer Hunter*, I thought, by way of *The Right Stuff* by way of *Mission: Impossible*.

Wombat told the story well, but sometimes a

look came into his eyes hinting that he knew we were playing games. Still, he sauntered forth, waving his thumbs in imaginary suspenders. "Pilgrum," he said. "I want you to take command of the Pepsi trailer."

We were the first to arrive. I looked across the stream of traffic, glimmering in the afternoon sun, toward the other rest stop. I nodded soberly. "All right, Cap'n," I said. "Somebody's gotta do it."

He scribbled down his cell phone number. "For commo checks."

"Roger that, sir." He liked that, the "sir."

I drove to the interchange, back on the other side, and opened the stand. I had one customer as I worked, a truck driver from West Virginia. He stared at our brochure, then looked doubtfully at me. "You were over there?"

"Sure was."

"You seem like a real normal guy."

"Thanks, I—"

"They gonna fly it in?"

"What?"

"Your turkey dinner! For turkey day!" He laughed at his own joke, then dug in his pockets and threw all his change in the bucket. He walked off laughing, and when he turned out with his truck gave thumbs up.

An old couple slowly approached, in a Lincoln with Ontario plates. They sat in the car several minutes, staring at the trailer, at me and my long, anachronistic hair. Finally they emerged and carefully walked by, not looking at me, the woman clinging to the man. I called Wombat.

"Read you loud and clear, guy. How you me?"

"Lickin chicken."

"Any customers?"

"Made a dollar."

"Real fine, soldier, real fine. Carry on."

Wombat was probably right that I looked pitiful. I'd come to Paradise to clear the air after my divorce. Old and weary as I was, I hoped to don a golden tan, make a killing in real estate, go adventuring among the Seminoles.

Instead I rented an apartment in the Cuban part of town and worked at three separate, and separately dead-end, jobs. I drove a beat-up Chevy and ate pot pies and before long, though I saved a wad of money, any distinction between myself and animals had blurred.

A year passed, then two, until finally my loneliness had a a sort of purity to it. Without planning to, I'd sorted things out. I wanted to live on a farm again, raise vegetables, and cut wood. I had a son up north, and perhaps I could be something for him. I could be available, at least.

My solace through that time had been the veterans. In my prosperous, youthful days I thought veterans were those pot-bellied old farts who wore funny hats and got drunk at Holiday Inns. They'd been cooks and supply sergeants but as the years passed they transformed themselves into heroes.

Alas, I'd lost my virginal blush. I, too, had become a veteran.

Wombat was married, but the rest of us were separated, divorced, broken up to the point where our frailties seemed forever damming. I had taken what comfort a man can in male company. As I poured coffee and scooped ice, and delivered the group's spiel about the noble sacrifices Vietnam vets had made, and how the public spurned them and the government let them down, the last thing on my mind was a woman.

She wore thick glasses, and her hair, drawn severely into a ponytail, was long and unruly. She had fair skin, and had taken a sunburn. Her car, a battle-scarred Mazda, shuddered as she drove up, and dieseled for fifteen seconds after she'd cut the engine.

She was like that, too: a bit out of time. She stepped gracefully from the car and would have turned any man's head but then, on the smooth asphalt, she stumbled, caught herself, and walked ahead so purposefully that the timid little girl shone through.

She joined me at the Pepsi stand, announcing she was here to help the veterans through the weekend. As she finished her speech her eyes leapt with surprise, as they met mine. She ducked her head but brought it up with a brave smile. For some of us, simply greeting the day took courage.

"I'm Silvie. Dawson's girl."

"Oh, right," I said, nodding. "The marine." Our hero, I thought, the man with the Navy Cross. I wondered if it would do any good to mention my Bronze Star—but I'd never stoop so low. "Good for Dawson," I murmured.

"Oh," Silvie said, neutrally, but drawing out the word. "Oh, I don't know."

In a few minutes, when *he* arrived, Silvie ran to throw her arms around him, and look up at him almost worshipfully. It was as if he were the leader of a cult. In fact, he did go to survivalist camps sometimes, and talked vaguely of becoming a mercenary in the Mideast.

He earned his Navy Cross at DaNang, laying down fire as wounded were evacuated. It was the only extraordinary thing that had ever happened to him, and he venerated it night and day. He drove a van he'd painted camouflage, and wore camouflage fatigues. A bull rattler's skin hung over his rearview mirror. He lived somewhere among the palmettos and cypresses of Pasco County, where, people said, black bears still roamed.

His van was filled with guns and knives and exercise machines. He was all energy. As he talked to you he made small, involuntary poses—turns of the neck, a flexing of his calf muscles—in a kind of martial dance. He always seemed about to say something significant, but sel-dom spoke, unless it were to defend our role in Vi-etnam long ago.

He and I argued at our first meeting. "The

fucking protesters," he said. "And worse than that, the politicians."

"They were right. We were caught in the middle, that's all."

"We were winning! All they talked about back in the World was Tet, Tet, Tet; but we had the VC with their pants down! Another year, the North would have been on its knees."

"What for? The only difference it would have made is you wouldn't have had Pol Pot, all that Khmer Rouge business."

"Okay. Okay. How many million did *they* kill?"

I nodded. Dawson and I went silent, and Wombat quickly changed the subject to the volunteer work we were doing at a Willie Nelson concert. Ever afterward, Dawson and I were uneasy with each other—though respectful, too, old soldiers vanquished by time.

I wondered what Silvie saw in him. I thought women liked sensitive, ironic men, such as myself. Then again, what did a divorced man know about women?

Gene Cooley, who had been with an armored unit in the Highlands and was badly burned up one side of his body and face from a freak explosion of C-4, arrived. He was a huge man, fat, and he smoked constantly. He was gentle, with grave Texas manners. Often his eyes were bloodshot. He worked nights at a convenience store.

Patriotism was his religion. He propped an American flag on the trailer, and it fell down. He spent half an hour securing it with duct tape, breathing heavily. Afterwards, he patrolled the entire rest stop perimeter, slow-moving as a turtle.

He peered into the swamp behind, and walked among the big rigs, and staggered in the sand along the Interstate, picking up some aluminum cans. I understood: you had to see where you were, assess avenues of attack, makes plans for the defense.

Satisfied at last, Gene popped a tape of the Doors into his car stereo, and sat on a beach chair behind the trailer. He begged a beer from the marine and started on a pack of Marlboros.

Meanwhile, Silvie gave every weary traveler a smile. She would smile, I thought, as you steadily broke her heart. Silvie and Dawson moved nicely together, an unlikely, perfect couple, as if she were the only person on earth for whom he could soften those hard edges, or she were the only person who could see those edges weren't really so hard.

And he caught her little vulnerabilities, made her less tentative if not exactly confident—ah, yes, I thought, there was hope. If I might have concluded, from my marriage, that only money mattered, here was a woman who'd give all she had to a man with nothing.

Around eight p.m.—or 2000 hours, as Wombat had it—the marine set up a gas grill and made hamburgers. I sat eating a cheeseburger with a handful of Hydrox cookies and some of the potato salad that Gene Cooley had brought, and which it would have been the deepest imaginable offense not to sample. We swilled the food down with Coors in cans, and then lay on the hillside in the warm night, under the big Florida moon, drinking, swapping stories, swatting the black flies and mosquitoes that swarmed out of the swamp.

Truckers pulled in to catch some sleep and when they woke stumbled over, at two or three in the morning. They held out their coffee cups like beggars seeking alms, then grabbed a handful of cookies, before heading on to Orlando or Ft. Pierce.

The janitor came out and stood near the grill long enough that Dawson made him a hamburger.

"How you like your job?" I asked.

"It's a hard job." He sighed and shook his head tragically. "Long weekend like this, we'll go through five cases of toilet paper."

"That's a lot of asses," the marine said, with a thin smile.

The janitor looked off across the highway. "You get some characters. I don't mean you, not you men. That thing you were in, nobody understood why, only nobody blamed you, neither."

Not exactly, I thought, glancing at the marine. He stood with his chin up, in profile against the moon.

The janitor swallowed coffee. "Sometimes, I say to Rita, if it wasn't for I'd mess up my retirement, we'd pull up stakes and head back to Tennessee. Nothin' down here no more. Tuesday night, maybe seven, eight in the evenin', we had these two nigra boys come up from Tampa. I thought, they look suspicious, but like I say to

Rita, a man should mind his own business, and anyhow you see so many. They sat out there smok-in' dope in an old beat-up three-quarter-ton Dodge, just waitin'.

"And finally, this old woman from New York City pulls up, and they run and got her purse. They lit out south. I called the *po*-lice, but see that's why they was on this side, they's an inter-change down two miles. They got off just when the highway patrol put down their coffee cups."

"Is there a lot of that kind of thing?" asked the marine, dropping his head, and looking stern.

"Naw. What you see mostly is the kids makin' their dope deals."

"Helluva world," the marine said.

It was 0400. We hadn't had a customer for an hour. Silvie had gone to sleep in the van, so whatever elegance or mystery the night held was gone. Gene lay snoring in his lawn chair, gas rumbling in his belly.

The marine's conversation, such as it was, grew impatient, and his eyes drifted toward the van. As he turned to join Silvie, and I rose to head for the knoll where I'd thrown out my sleeping bag, a white Mercedes two-door with tinted glass streaked in, trailing smoke.

Gene woke, exactly as if the perimeter had been breached, and raised himself from his chair. The three of us jumped like a pit crew.

A woman—a blonde in a white, lowcut summer dress and white stockings—leaped from the Mercedes, saw us, and made a mute, helpless female appeal. Except in the movies, I'd never seen one. The fire was real, the damsel's distress was real, but still she had to turn it all into an *act*.

Fine with us. The marine, when he saw the car coming, ran to his van to grab an extinguisher, while Gene, like a great, clumsy bird, waved his arms to fan away smoke. "Yes, Ma'am, yes, Ma'am. Stand back, Ma'am," he said, as the lady in white stamped her feet, and turned about in panic.

I thought the problem was under the hood— maybe a ruptured fuel line—and remembered some training from somewhere: raise the hood only enough to use your extinguisher. But this wasn't an engine fire. My nose caught the sizzle and stench of a burning tire.

The marine took the glories, dousing the fire in three long bursts of CO_2. He stepped back, and stood almost at attention.

"*Won*-derful," said the woman in white. "I'd don't know what I'd have done if—"

I came around with a jack and her spare, but Gene yanked them from me and dropped to the cement. On his belly, he sought out a niche for the jack. It was clear he didn't want any help, and I stepped back and smiled at the woman—very pretty. Very out of my league.

Silvie climbed from the van and walked slowly over, looking nearsighted and frail without her glasses, and unglamorous alongside the visitor.

She stared at the woman in white and looped her arm around the marine. The woman edged toward me, second choice.

What the hell. Once you give up, things aren't so bad.

"Out late," I said.

The woman bit her lip. Her prettiness, like her act of distress, didn't quite convince. "I have to be in Ocala for a friend's party. And I couldn't get away, couldn't get away—you know how it is."

"Afraid I don't get out much any more."

This seemed to offend her, because she snapped off her reply: "It's *your* fault if you don't."

Very much out of my league. But it struck me that women such as Silvie were more rare.

Gene clawed his way up the fender, and leaned against it, panting. "Crank it, Irish," he called out irritably. Of course, the engine and the tire were unrelated, but I slid behind the wheel for solidarity's sake. The engine started easily, and I raced it a little, before dropping it back to an idle. Nice machine. Also out of my league.

The woman in white applauded.

"Used to work on tractors," Gene announced, still panting, but with authority. He rolled the damaged tire toward the trunk, and heaved it inside.

"Amazing," said the woman in white. She pulled a red shawl around her tanned shoulders, gathered her skirt, and slid behind the wheel.

"Mmm," she said, and brushed Gene's scarred cheek with her fingers. "Thank you."

"Really nice car," he said, fighting for breath. "I wonder if, you wanta keep it nice, maybe you oughtta drive a little slower."

"I will. I promise." She put the Mercedes in gear and edged forward.

"You're the most beautiful—" Gene began, but his voice faltered, and the woman gave no sign she heard.

"Your man," she called to Silvie. "He's a real hero!"

"I think they're *all* heroes," Silvie said, running a hand across Dawson's hard chest.

I was so weary I could hardly climb to the knoll, and sleep. But I felt good about myself, I think because I had belonged somewhere for a little while.

Sleep came like a steep fall, and I was with my father when he was a young man still, and I was as small as my own son. Dad was making me a bow out of Osage Orange, the hardest and toughest wood in the United States, wood that always springs erect. We were out in the shop on a winter day and the barrel stove sizzled, but wind rattled the windows, and the cement floor was cold. After a while, somehow, I took my father's place, and whittled patiently at that bow with a spoke shave, while the boy looking up became my son.

I awoke on the hillside to the birds singing with dawn, my legs stiff, this foreign land of Florida so hot that already I was panting, and sitting by my side was Sylvie.

"Good morning, Irish," she said. "I have something for you." She held out a cup of coffee and a breakfast biscuit from McDonald's.

"Dawson bought it for you."

"Thanks," I said. "Where's the—where is Dawson?"

"He went to Tampa for ice."

"You sleep?"

"A little. After all the excitement—"

"Did he sleep?"

"He . . . yes. He doesn't sleep much."

"Ever vigilant."

"What?"

I stood slowly, testing my aching knees. I kicked out one foot and then the other. I was too old to sleep on the ground. "It's pretty good, the two of you?"

She hesitated. "He found me, I was coming apart. He—"

"You see that truck there? Brand-new truck?"

She smiled, and I wanted to grab her up and run, marine or no marine. "Sure. Dawson says you're going home."

"Let's take a ride. Let's take a long ride."

She laughed. "Where to, bigshot?"

"Alaska!"

"You're terrible. You're not serious."

"Of course not," I said, looking away. I couldn't find words for a moment. "It's great, he's got somebody like you."

"And I have somebody like *him*." She brought up her chin. "You'll find someone, Irish."

"Right." We reached the Pepsi trailer, and I poured more coffee, and ate a cookie.

Wombat called. "Make boocoo dinero, did you?"

"Not quite two hundred. You?"

"Same-same. We got three more days. Talk to you later, big guy."

There was a flurry of customers, and Sylvie and I worked side by side. Without looking at me she said, "Did you win any medals over there?"

"Win!"

"I mean, I mean . . . *award*."

"Not me. I'm a boy wonder, not a hero."

She smiled. Gene Cooley woke and headed for the bathroom, tucking in his shirttail as he walked. The janitor shuffled by, nodded, and went home.

Dawson returned with ice and twelve dozen doughnuts, and managed what for him was a big smile. I was headed north again, a little richer, maybe a little wiser, ready for fatherhood and even romance. It occurred to me that this was Thanksgiving Day.

My Vietnam:
An Afterward

I WROTE about half of these stories in the mid-1980s, during a period when my dad died, my marriage ended, and I was hounded out of a job.

Given my troubles, it was ironic how easy the stories were to publish—in good quarterlies and in what used to be called "slicks," or magazines with high circulation. Some of them were gathered up in a small press publication, *Tanks*. The title story actually won a Missouri-wide contest, and generated movie interest with the great critic, Pauline Kael. (Very old news, but she was out in Hollywood as a guest of Warren Beatty, trying to put some money where her mouth was. She wanted to call "Tanks," "Frag.")

I thought I was on my way. It took me a while to realize that I'd written the stories during the brief—the only—boom in Vietnam fiction, when well-known novels such as *Paco's Story* (Larry Heinemann) and *The 13th Valley* (John Del Vecchio) were published.

Other stories—and my novel, *Soldier in Paradise*—came along after the boom, and proved quite difficult to publish. By then it was clear I wouldn't become famous or make any money to speak of.

I'm not complaining. It's just that maybe the stories don't deserve an afterward in the usual sense—that is, I'd be dead and somebody else would do the writing.

However, since this is a self-published effort, I I can have an afterward if I want one—and, afterward or forward, these are pretty good stories. The early ones—"Tanks," or "Hot,"—give an honest impression of combat, and those written in the 1990s catch some of the life-long unease that was the special lot of Vietnam veterans.

I wish my characters hadn't smoked so much dope, or gone into the bushes with prostitutes quite so often, but I resisted the temptation to sanitize these stories. I cut some clunky writing, sharpened the internal logic here and there, and reordered some paragraphs, but I stayed in the spirit of the younger writer, simply acting as his editor.

The combat stories were the first thing I wrote that was any good. By pulling together the best of them, and carefully revising them, I mean to put to rest important parts of my life and career. Therefore, an afterward makes some sense.

More: George Hobson, commander of C/2/8 way back when, contacted me to contribute to a book he's putting together on the company. This piece began that way—and without George's efforts, I would not have had access to some very striking photos.

What follows is the nonfiction background to the stories, sort of answering the questions all writers hate, "What really happened?" and "Is this true?" (See Tim O'Brien's "How to Tell a True War Story.")

The war was so long ago, in other words, that I can't remember anything with perfect accuracy, so what follows, like fiction, is only approximate truth. But even approximate truth, when you're dealing with a big, slippery subject such as war, is superior to indisputable facts.

In 1965 I began college in North Manchester, Indiana, at a Church of the Brethren school with a fine reputation. I was a fake Hoosier, however, having spent most of my childhood on little farms in southern Missouri—e.g., "Good Blood."

I had long hair and rode a motorcycle, and might have seemed a romantic figure. But I was really just a transplanted hillbilly, scared of girls, chronically shy, ignorant and naïve.

Rather like their cousins, the Mennonites— and like the better-known Quakers—the Brethren are pacifists. I developed a lot of respect for them.

They operated the Brethren Voluntary Service, or BVS, which did—still does—VISTA-like work throughout the country. BVS was one way of getting out of the draft. The kids who joined BVS didn't believe war was justified, any war, and those I knew were utterly sincere.

Listening to rants on both sides of the question, it didn't seem to me that the Vietnam War made much sense. A lot of men were dying for what at best seemed like a chess match between Robert McNamara and General Giap. The Domino Theory? What was that? Where were the Huns, or the Nazis, carrying off our fair virgins?

Then there was Jane Fonda, posing prettily on North Vietnamese anti-aircraft guns. It was a real betrayal, particularly for the horny fans of *Barbarella*—many of whom were serving in Vietnam.

(However, my personal characterization of Fonda is revisionist; I hardly understood her politics at the time, and didn't see Barbarella *until I reached Vietnam. I did indeed agonize over my feelings about war.)*

Fonda's antics dovetailed with the anti-war rhetoric characterizing President Johnson as a baby-burner and war criminal. Johnson was trapped by the policies of Kennedy and Eisenhower before him. The man was overbearing, arrogant, crooked, but a war criminal? He got the Civil Rights bill through. He didn't *start* the damn war. He kept upping the ante with troops and bombing because he wanted out of it.

And he was a hillbilly like me. Witness his holding up those hound dogs by the ears, and speeding down the dusty red roads of the Texas hill country in his Lincoln Continental.

I could have hung back a bit longer, until the lottery began, and perhaps have escaped the war. In the end, I took a middling route: I dropped out of college, and volunteered for the draft. I didn't really belong with those nice kids in the BVS. Already, I knew I wanted to be a writer. It was a bad war, but it was also the biggest story of my generation.

In the fall of 1968, down at Ft. Campbell for basic training, I drew an old yahoo drill sergeant who was certainly tough, but he also was—how do I put it?—full of love.

Toward the end of training, one morning around four a.m., the lights came on. They had begun to relax their manic discipline somewhat, so, as I stared into the glare, I wondered what we'd done to merit losing sleep. Oh, God, I thought: another cold run. More screaming at me over breakfast. More vomiting.

A fierce, toothy head dangled before me, its fur caked with dried blood.

"Hit's a bobcat, boys!" our drill sergeant said. "Shot him right on the fort here!"

The guy *likes* us, I suddenly realized. He had to show his bobcat to his boys.

The same man—a hillbilly, you understand, like my secret soul—stood on the PT stand one sunny morning, put the three platoons at ease, and demonstrated how to tie a tie, explaining every step in his Tennessee drawl. He was precise. It was impossible not to learn. I've had a couple of jobs where I wore a tie every day, and always I thought, "Thanks a lot, Drill Sergeant."

I reported to Ft. Lewis for Advanced Infantry Training (AIT), along with Tim Hildebrandt, an artist from Logansport, Indiana. More about Tim later.

AIT was a big bore except for the Escape and Evasion course. The drill instructors didn't have the gravitas of that old hillbilly at Ft. Campbell, but they hyped the thing endlessly. It would go on all night, as you thrashed through the woods from the point of escape to Checkpoint Charley, all along being harassed by the enemy. God help you if you were captured. They'd put you in a cage and poke sticks at you.

We were all pretty cynical by then. There's not much romance in being a conscript for an unpopular war.

Somewhere I found a map on which the Escape and Evasion course was clearly outlined, right up against a state highway. To the south, almost adjacent to the course, was a little town called Roy. So on the night of our trial, when our leaders pointed north toward Checkpoint Charley and shooed us into the woods, I convinced Tim and another man to accompany me out of the bounds of the course, and into Roy.

There was nothing to see there, but a general store was open, and we bought a six-pack of Olympia. The air was chilly and none of us really wanted the beer, but it seemed to enhance our outlaw exploits.

Then we walked up the state highway, parallel to all the excitement. There was a big moon and plenty of stars, so we could see blanks going off, explosions, intense lights, and at last a truck growling through the Douglas firs, carrying prisoners in a cage.

Kind of like one of those haunted houses cities put up at Halloween.

We sat drinking in the woods across the highway, hardly one hundred meters from Checkpoint Charley. The escapees who had evaded the harassment, but who had the temerity to report in first, got harassed still further, and were thrown into the cage. Not fair, we thought, but as more soldiers straggled in, we saw that the harassment tapered off. Around four a.m. we crossed the road, slipped behind another group, and got ourselves cups of coffee.

We were the best escapees and evaders of all, but couldn't tell anyone.

At Bien Hoa, as I awaited assignment, a first sergeant swept me up with two others, and set us to digging a ditch. I asked what was it for, and the first sergeant said, "Drainage."

Digging the ditch to nowhere, or digging the meaningless hole, is famous World War II lore, but I couldn't believe such silliness still went on. The first sergeant was pleasant and chatted with us a while, and we thought the project was real.

I'd worked on a lot of construction jobs, so wielding a shovel was kind of fun. The first sergeant said he'd never seen such a fine shoveler, and it's probably true. It's not much to claim, but I'm good with a shovel.

Then the day grew hot, and the first sergeant left—saying he'd bring us some water. The water didn't arrive, and the other men climbed from the ditch. "Enough of this bullshit," said one. I shoveled on for a while, but then crawled out, too, and headed for the PX. I'd been conned. It truly was a ditch to nowhere.

There I was, as we used to say, taken in by the oldest and dumbest ploy the army had to offer. I'd been conned because I didn't believe anybody could be so stupid as to suggest such a stupid task.

The first sergeant taught me a lesson, though I'm not quite sure what it was. Maybe it's, *when confronted with stupidity, don't outsmart yourself.*

Tim Hildebrandt and I were linked again in our first assignment. I can't remember where it was—up country somewhere, in rolling terrain spotted with fields of grass, shallow lagoons, and scrub timber. Reminded me of Florida.

Guys who had been in-country a while weren't especially friendly. It was as though they belonged to a fraternity, and you'd been pledged, but they wouldn't explain the rules for full membership.

A no-nonsense sergeant from Louisiana, a black man who could barely read, made a project of me, and probably kept me alive. I wish I could remember his name. He didn't like the army much, but he was a fine soldier.

We flew out from the LZ on platoon-sized patrols. Wearisome stuff, and nothing happened for several weeks. Then one night just before dawn I woke to the booms of Claymores, and rifle fire. Twigs and mud and little stones—and dried fish—rained down in the camp. As daylight came, we counted the North Vietnamese dead. There might have been three, or six, I can't recall.

Our casualty was Tim. He pranced around the camp, delighted he was going home, and talking crazy talk. "I got a million dollar wound," he said, pointing to the back of his head. A piece of shrapnel had pierced his skull.

Sure enough, he went home, and I had several letters from him. Later, Tim and his brother, Greg, became the famous Hildebrandt Brothers, a team of fantasy illustrators who produced, among many other things, the Lord of the Rings calendars of the 1970s, and the first Star Wars poster.

But Tim suffered a great deal before that. He spent a year at Ft. Riley, sweeping up the entire fort to hear him tell it. Then surgeons put a steel plate in his skull, and the army released him. But the wound had aggravated his childhood dyslexia, so that for a long time he couldn't find perspective in his painting—and therefore, couldn't work.

Tim died in 2006.

<<>>

After the skirmish, the old guys accepted me, and tried me out at point.

I was a failure, but not, strictly speaking, because I was afraid. Some men, such as the late Gene Dunn, seemed to have an instinct for pointing, maybe because they'd done a lot of hunting. I stared before me, and was paralyzed. Suddenly, all the world was my responsibility. If you missed a suspicious arrangement in the weeds, or a movement or sound, somebody could get killed. It was all too difficult for me.

Here was the material, I suppose, that eventually resulted in "Called of God." I wrote the story at a Burger King in Lakeland, Florida, as my father was dying.

They put me to carrying ammo, and then the squad RTO went home, and I replaced him. I was a fine RTO. I spoke clearly and didn't get rattled. I moved up to the platoon slot, and toward the end of my tour became Jade's—Captain Joe Gesker's—battalion RTO. I'd found something I could do well, and be proud of.

Norm Gipe tells me we used to sit in foxholes and write stories on C-ration cardboard—he one sentence, me the next. I don't remember this, but I know I was always scribbling something, and I read constantly, carrying paperbacks my mom sent that, altogether, must have weighed ten pounds. I wrapped the one I was currently reading in plastic inside a LRP (Long Range Patrol) container, and carried that in a deep side pocket, and read through the day as we labored along. Even with my precautions against the monsoon, the books got wet. I'd peel off pages and leave them for the edification of the North Vietnamese—Dickens, Tolstoy, Dreiser. I liked the classics because they went on so long.

Norm and I sang songs as we walked through the brush, in that high whisper that was sort of allowed. The songs I remember most are Jackie DeShannon's "Put a Little Love in Your Heart," and the Beatles' "Baby, You Can Drive My Car." Imagine singing such songs when you're soaked in sweat, and brush keeps swatting you in the face, and your legs are shot, and your pack straps bear down like you're carrying an anvil. Then all of a sudden, up the column somewhere, there's incoming, and word comes back that someone's dead.

Speaking of music, one of the few vets I saw after the war, the late Ralph Bianculli, aka "New York," had been in a band called The Good Rats. The army was putting together a band down in Bien Hoa, to entertain on aircraft carriers—and LZs, too, I guess.

Ralph was a flamboyant guy, and quite the operator. He kept claiming how he'd applied to play in that band, and it was only a matter of time before he'd be on easy street. I said, right, like that's gonna happen. But it did, to the amazement—one might say, the *awe*—of everyone in the company.

Headed out for R. & R., I heard Ralph's band in Bien Hoa, practicing in an unused barracks. They played, "Dear Prudence," and were damn good. Much later, Ralph joined Gene Dunn in a West Texas band, and they played small venues in places like Lubbock, and then over in the gas country of New Mexico. I'm sorry I didn't get to hear them.

One of my most surreal memories is also one I can place in time: Christmas Day, 1969.

We humped all morning through some rugged terrain, finally descending into a wooded valley that in its deepest portion had been blasted clear from a B-52 strike. We set up around a crater that had formed a little lake, and had a flat berm on one side where helicopters could land.

They proceeded to fly in those oval Mermite cans containing our Christmas dinner, and we lined up for turkey and barely warm mashed potatoes and so forth, deep in the jungle. Then another chopper landed, and out stepped a navy glee club in their immaculate whites, and gave us a kind of Brothers Four rendition of "God Rest Ye Merry Gentleman" and "Tannenbaum."

The navy flew away, and the Mermite cans disappeared without an opportunity for seconds. Another bird circled. It was a Chieu Hoi helicopter, which ordinarily spewed out American propaganda, but they'd rigged it to play Bing

Crosby's "White Christmas."

Let's say they were 800 meters up. Bing's voice was distorted, so that you could only make out the melody, and a high-powered, scary gargling. Like a tape playing backward, but loud. Must have frightened a lot of geckos.

I wasn't entertained, or disgusted, or amused. I couldn't comprehend it.

I have no idea where this was, or when. Some of us flew out with combat engineers to blow up an LZ that had been overrun. I don't know how many men were killed, and how many extracted.

We threaded up a long field, wary that some of the enemy might still be lurking in the woods. Here and there smoke rose, but mostly fires had burned themselves out. I recall an overturned, burned-out "mule"—those little flatbed trucks.

Several went ahead to check for booby traps, but there didn't appear to be any; and the engineers began setting charges. We fanned out over the little base, looking for small, salvageable objects.

The place was a ghost town. Overturned ammo boxes lay scattered with empty water cans, clothing, and busted chairs. You knew a terrible struggle had gone on, and if you raised your eyes toward that ominously near wood line, you got chills.

A ragged tarp fluttered over what must have been the mess hall, and several of us made our way there, hoping for food to scrounge. Up on a table, like some kind of abandoned offering, sat a round, massive block of cheese. The skin hadn't been pierced, and it was stamped with those black, block style army letters, "Wisconsin Cheddar Cheese." Or maybe the words read, "Cheese, Cheddar, Wisconsin." The cheese was three feet across, and four feet high.

How did this fine, perishable thing make its way from Wisconsin to such a godforsaken spot? You'd have thought it would have been diverted in the rear somewhere, and fed to generals. It was too good for the poor grunts who'd bled and died for it. They never even tasted it.

And what of the North Vietnamese? Didn't they like cheese?

"It's spoiled," I remember saying.

A soldier pulled out his knife and cut a sample. "No," he said. "It's great."

Word came the engineers had finished their work, and it was time to pull back. Oh, no, I thought. The cheese!

I sawed off a pound or two, and others rushed in like rats, and maybe we accounted for a tenth of that big block. We marched up the field, and the LZ blew up impressively as we wolfed down cheese. Oh, for some decent bread, and some wine!

We tried our best to kill them—the ones designated as our enemies—but grunts hardly knew any Vietnamese. You spent a year in the country, but learned little about it. I wanted to go to Saigon, for instance, and never could. Soldiers who actually learned something about Vietnam were probably not in combat.

For a while, we had an ARVN scout assigned to us. Everyone said he was worthless—everyone said *all* the ARVNs were worthless—but I tried to get to know this guy. His name was something like "Tru Vu." I'd say hi to him in the mornings, and he'd say hi back. He was married, I learned, and wrote poetry in the classic Vietnamese manner.

He was indeed a lousy scout. While I don't remember the details, I know that he, at least indirectly, led us into an ambush. Not long after that, he fell behind the column, and when they heard a thrashing, the squad following last shot him dead. Accidentally? Accidentally, on purpose? Lots of things happened like the death of Tru Vu, and you never knew the truth. But no one, including the captain, seemed to grieve Tru Vu's passing.

Our more usual contact with the Vietnamese was with camp followers—a wonderful term historically, and in politics, but in this case referring to "boom-boom girls"—a pretty wonderful term, too. Five dollah one time, twenty dollah all night.

Enough said.

But to bring up yet another compromising subject, there was a lot of drug use among soldiers. A lot of rock music, a lot of partying. Our behavior was particularly reckless on an LZ called Barbara, which supposedly had been built by the French. It was the Hilton of LZs, with electric lights in the bunkers, and real bunks. Soldiers sat up top in chaise longues made of sand bags—and *tripped,* to use the language of the time. They played guitars, and studied the night sky, and held forth on profound subjects. We were young men, far adrift, and it seemed no one cared about us.

Sometimes, there would be a "mad minute," and the sky would light up, and red and green tracers would crisscross, and maybe a barrel of Fougas would blow. Wild stuff.

A lot of marijuana got smoked. I never saw anyone use it in the field though alcohol was consumed—after dark, on guard. Friends sent whiskey—which sometimes made it through the mail room. The army itself often supplied beer— Pabst, and Carling Black Label. I could trade beer for my own passion, C-ration apricots.

Some soldiers claimed there was a lot of heroin use in the rear areas. They said the Thai soldiers brought it in. They said some of those RATs (Rear Action Trash) kept extending their tours because they were addicts. These stories were akin to urban legends, a folklore impossible to verify, though I was fascinated by it.

The drug use suggested a demoralized army. We knew the war was shutting down, and that nothing had been resolved. In the 1970s, a lot of embittered veterans would say, "We never lost a battle." Nonetheless, the war tore the country apart, and the public seemed to hate us.

< < > >

I was in the bush almost my entire tour, and never wounded, but I developed a massive, thoroughly disgusting boil (See "Hot") on my neck, and after that, an aggressive case of jungle rot. The medic—and he was a fine medic—blamed me for it, which I resented. I changed to dry socks when I could get them, but you lived in the rain, and your feet were wet hours on end. I always took his medicine religiously—the horse pill for malaria, the anti-fungal pills for jungle rot.

At first, the pills worked a cure, and the jungle rot retreated. But since the conditions didn't change, the jungle rot returned, and after a while the pills didn't work any more. It got so bad I could hardly walk, no matter how I padded my feet or how carefully I laced up my boots. Pissed off, the medic set me up for a profile, and I joined the troupe of shammers at battalion headquarters, in Tay Ninh.

If you were wounded and in the hospital, that was an honorable thing. Blue-eyed blondes would visit you. But if you joined the twilight world of shammers, you were a leper. No one believed you were really sick. You were doing your best to avoid combat, and that was cowardly—if sensible.

Jungle rot seemed to be the chief among our maladies, but others recuperated from broken bones, minor wounds, malaria, and gonorrhea. (See "Incubation Period.") We mustered every morning, five of us or ten, and the first sergeant assigned details—usually not KP, because Vietnamese women did that, and most of us couldn't scamper around well enough for such work. We pulled night duty on the greenline—the bunkers around the LZ—but not frequently. The only regular duty I recall was burning shit.

There isn't a euphemism for it: we burned shit. You dragged out half barrels, half full, from the latrine, mixed in diesel fuel, and set the mixture on fire with a bit of toilet paper. You stirred it with a hoe, and maybe added more fuel, and that's all there was to it.

Necessary, of course. And I grew almost to like burning shit, because it took a while to get the job done, and no one bothered me. I'd sit on the berm, out of the way of the ghastly smoke, and read Charles Dickens.

When I finished burning shit, I liked to go down to the Filipino compound, where I'd be hard to find if some other duty arose. I could buy a cold San Miguel beer there, and read. Sometimes, I went to the Red Cross Club, where the Doughnut Dollies led us in their strange games.

After perhaps three weeks I returned to the field. It had stopped raining, and I managed to keep the jungle rot at bay.

Some of those guys, however, would open a wound to keep from returning. They saw no point whatever in the war. Morale wasn't high for any of us, but for the dedicated shammer, the idea of "morale" wasn't even on the planet.

<<>>

The biggest battle I lived through occurred on Valentine's Day, 1970. Before long, I would go home. I had just moved to the CP (Command Position), joining Captain Gesker as his battalion RTO. The platoon I left behind, Log Chain, would be decimated—essentially, wiped out. For survivors of that battle, it's our most difficult memory.

I wrote about this back in the 1980s, in a long story called "Tanks." I don't want to write about it again, but I thought I might round out the picture a little by reminding veterans of what happened about three hours before the battle.

Charley was attached to an armored unit, which was hard for us. We had to ride up on top on that steel plate, and it bruised your bones. The armored soldiers were a different breed, and partied all night. Loud noises were their specialty. In my story, the armored commander is a baldheaded jerk, and I doubt that he was. I don't remember him at all. But the command structure was a little confusing, because there were two commanders.

The armored soldiers lost men, too. The remnants of that company, wherever they are, also have terrible memories.

There are several characters named in the following excerpt, but they aren't based on anyone. "Porter" is pretty clearly me.

The story opens at dawn. The tracks have camped out in the middle of a big field. Here and there, soldiers are winding in their Claymores.

Men are waking up, and staggering to the mess track for breakfast and coffee. The following occurs when "Porter" returns to his bedroll:

He saw a crane. It was huge, with a white neck; except for the black tips of its white wings, it was white. With the early sun, the damp-looking jungle, it suggested a cool pastoral; its wings seemed to sweep in time with the rolling grass. It flew low, ponderously . . . correct. "Caree . . . caree . . . " it sang.

It crossed the sun, and the sun, too, was correct: wild and orange and over-sized, holding the crane. There had been such moments in Missouri, on land so backward Porter thought he was the first to come calling . . .

"Jesus," Okie said, softly. The three of them had stood to watch the crane. Then the dream was over: Billy Boy raised his rifle, thumbed it to automatic, let fly six rounds.

Porter was amazed. Of course! If you had a gun you could shoot it. It hadn't occurred to him. Stunned, he nodded stupidly as Preacher stepped forward, raised a hand like a prophet, and shouted, "Don't shoot that bird!"

But all the perimeter had the idea. Men leaped up on the tanks and wheeled the .50 Calibers around. The morning roared alive. The crane flew past the sun, seemed to hang in the air before a dead tree, the only one on the plain.

Then it fell. Officers ran up, to protest the firing, but it had already ceased.

The crane—an egret, I suppose, though in my mind's eye the bird is much larger than an egret—did exist, and we did shoot it down. I don't believe there was a soldier called "Preacher," but a lot of soldiers were devout Christians, and possibly I based this character on a nice Mormon kid whose name I can't remember. (He was later killed.)

Being a literary wonk, I was attempting to evoke "The Rime of the Ancient Mariner," Coleridge's poem, in which a sailor kills an albatross representing good luck and a pure, serene spirit. After the albatross is killed, all hell breaks loose.

I returned from the war to Ft. Carson, where I had a bit of luck, and became a company clerk. I'd been promoted to sergeant, and thus didn't have to pull KP, and I was excused also from field maneuvers. A lot of the guys from Charley popped up around the base, and some would drop by, and tell me how much they hated those maneuvers. It was impossible to motivate a draftee who'd already served in Vietnam, and had only a few months of service remaining. James Patrick Cafferty, aka Irish, perhaps the fiercest soldier I ever knew, just couldn't handle garrison duty.

I recall one soldier, I'll call him Danny though I don't remember his name, who stormed into the CQ one morning, and scuffled with the XO. Danny was in the wrong, but believe me, the XO was no prince.

Anyhow, I filled out a report on Danny, not understanding the implications, and the upshot was that I had to strap on a .45 and escort him to the stockade. The stockade was terrifying. I was almost in tears. Danny was a nice guy, and had been through hell in Vietnam. He had a wife and child to support. His problem was debt, and his creditors were coming after him through the XO.

Nonetheless, I liked my time in Colorado. A girlfriend came to see me, and we went up into the mountains. I almost re-enlisted—I'd go to officer school, or get some medical training. But the times were wrong for it, and I couldn't get past my bitterness quickly enough. It took me a long time to realize that the war wasn't the army's fault.

Vietnam vets were all but criminalized in the public imagination, fed by the media. How many episodes of *Hawaii Five-O* were there, exactly, featuring a crazed veteran in a bell tower? You might as well blame the Japanese for their tsunami, but that wasn't something you could communicate, at least on a college campus. I didn't want to spend my life in argument. I did want an education, and I said very little.

Most of us went to work, got married, established careers. Maybe we were troubled by memories of the war, but we soldiered on.

After a while, the mood changed. Sometimes, we were victims to be pitied. Then novels and memoirs, and finally movies, appeared, presenting us in a better light. We changed from criminals to victims to dark heroes. They began to romanticize us, as in the Rambo movies.

I met a couple of teachers who told of their exploits in Vietnam—but they'd never been there. Imitation is flattery, I suppose.

The Vietnam Veterans Memorial helped a lot.

And now we've replaced the veterans of World War II, who are mostly gone. Whatever you think of our ongoing wars, seemingly the public has learned not to blame the soldiers. Even Jane Fonda—who, like all of us, is no longer a cute young thing—said she was sorry.

I wasn't wounded, and couldn't claim to have suffered from PTSD. I winced when I heard the wings of National Guard helicopters, beating over the horizon. I'm still startled by loud noises, or people coming up behind me. That's about it.

I joined a tour to Vietnam several years ago, and finally visited Saigon. It's a bustling place full of air pollution. The government maintains some war shrines, and dutifully stocks them with propaganda—and bored clerks. But the population is young, born long after the war, and pays no attention. They work in factories making clothing and cars to export to the West.

As tourists, we felt neither hostility nor friendliness. To my mind the *pho* tastes better in Houston, or Sacramento.

Speaking only for myself, the war turned out to be an asset. Because of the G.I. Bill, I got a good education. I wrote two books with a Vietnam War theme—well-regarded books. In recent years, I've reconnected with men I served with, and that's a joy. The war profoundly changed me, matured me, made it clear just how small and inconsequential I am. It gave me a deep appreciation for simple pleasures. I look back on it with wonder, and revulsion, and gratitude.

<<>>

John Mort

John Mort's first novel, *Soldier in Paradise* (1999), was widely reviewed and won the W. Y. Boyd Award for best military fiction. Other books include *Christian Fiction: A Guide to the Genre* (2002), and *Read the High Country: A Guide to Westerns* (2006), and *Goat Boy of the Ozarks* (2011), a novel.

Mort served with the First Cavalry as a point man and RTO, 1969-1970. He lives in Missouri.

<<>>

CPSIA information can be obtained at www.ICGtesting.com
Printed in the USA
BVOW03s1415141013

333699BV00007B/50/P